DREAMS *on*
MERSEY SQUARE

BOOKS BY PAM HOWES

THE MERSEY TRILOGY
The Lost Daughter of Liverpool
The Forgotten Family of Liverpool
The Liverpool Girls

LARK LANE SERIES
The Factory Girls of Lark Lane
The Shop Girls of Lark Lane
The Nurses of Lark Lane
The Midwives of Lark Lane

THE BRYANT SISTERS SERIES
The Girls of Victory Street
Wedding Bells on Victory Street
The Mothers of Victory Street
The Daughters of Victory Street
A Royal Visit to Victory Street

MERSEY SQUARE SERIES
The Girls of Mersey Square
The Mothers of Mersey Square
The Daughters of Mersey Square
Secrets on Mersey Square

A Child For Sale

Fast Movin' Train
Hungry Eyes
It's Only Words

DREAMS *on* MERSEY SQUARE

PAM HOWES

bookouture

Published by Bookouture in 2024

An imprint of Storyfire Ltd.
Carmelite House
50 Victoria Embankment
London EC4Y 0DZ

www.bookouture.com

First published as *Not Fade Away* by Cantello Publications in 2013.

ISBN: 978-1-83790-992-6
eBook ISBN: 978-1-83790-991-9

This book is dedicated to all the readers who became fans of my fictional group, The Raiders. I'm thrilled that you took my boys to your hearts like they are 'real' stars. Thank you.

PROLOGUE

When Roy Cantello, lead singer with chart-topping band The Raiders, had a brief affair with Livvy Grant, a young singer half his age, it was to change his and wife Sammy's lives forever. Roy fathered a daughter. Livvy handed baby Harley to him and Sammy to bring up as their own and then vanished from their lives, only to reappear when Harley was sixteen. Roy became re-involved with Livvy and when she claimed to be pregnant again with his child, Sammy divorced him. The child wasn't Roy's, but the son of Livvy's late husband, Daniel McVey. Roy has raised Danny as his own son. He and Livvy had a son, Roy Junior, the following year but their relationship failed as Roy was still in love with Sammy. Roy remarried Sammy six months ago and shares joint custody of the two little boys with Livvy. Everything is now warm and cosy in Roy's world, but not for long...

ALDERLEY EDGE, CHESHIRE, MAY 2005

Roy swatted a wasp from the neck of his lager bottle and pushed his shades up on top of his head. 'Bloody nuisance,' he muttered, wafting after the wasp with his newspaper. 'Bit of sun and they come out in swarms.'

'A single wasp's hardly a swarm,' his wife, Sammy, said. She stopped watering the patio planters as the wasp buzzed angrily around his head. She batted it away and it flew round to the front of him.

'See, there's another one!'

She shook her head, laughing. 'It's the same one, you dope! You're turning into a right grumpy old sod, Cantello! And besides, wasps don't swarm. It's bees that swarm.'

'Really?'

'Really.'

'Aren't you the clever one?' He smacked her playfully on the backside. 'Less of the old, you, and I'm not grumpy. Don't you remember how I nearly swallowed a wasp once when I was abroad with the band? The little bugger got in my lager can. Next thing it's stinging my bloody tongue and I couldn't sing that night. I could have swallowed it. Might have proved fatal.'

Sammy sat down on a lounger beside him. 'Yes, but it didn't and you're still here to tell the tale. Did you get the barbecue out of the garage? Is there any gas in the can?'

'Yep. I'll light it in a minute. They'll be getting hungry, I promised them hot dogs.' He dropped his shades back down his nose and looked across the well-tended garden to the play area, where RJ and Danny were in the sandpit, squabbling over whose turn it was to play with the digger. Never in his wildest dreams did he envisage having two under-fours at the age of sixty-one; running around after them kept him fit though. He looked at Sammy, who was watching the boys closely. He knew what she was thinking – well, at least he thought he did. She glanced at him and he reached for her hand and squeezed it. She had a nostalgic look on her face and sadness in her eyes. He swallowed hard, wished he could make it go away permanently. But it would take time, maybe the rest of his life. He'd never give up trying to make amends though. Sammy was his world, he'd love her forever.

'Wish we could go back in time,' she said wistfully.

'Me too. But you're happy, aren't you, Sam? I mean, with what we've got now? There's nowhere on earth I'd rather be than with you in this place.'

'And me, but don't you think the cottage is a bit too small when we have the boys to stay over? I really wish now that I'd hung on to Jasmine House. I was too hasty in selling it.' She was referring to their old Edwardian marital home. 'I miss all those spacious rooms and the huge garden. This cottage was supposed to be for my retirement. It's not big enough for a family. We can't stay here when the boys get older, we'll have to buy another house.'

'We'll see. Here's Harley.' He waved at his daughter, who emerged from the French doors and joined them on the sunloungers. 'How did the scan go, sweetheart?'

'Great,' Harley said. 'Everything's on track. Ten more weeks to go.' She rubbed her very pregnant belly. 'I'll never get up off this lounger, you're gonna have to get a crane.'

'Still only two in there?' he teased.

'Dad!' She laughed. 'Very funny. There's hardly room for two, never mind more.'

'We'll definitely need more space when the babies arrive,' Sammy said. 'Perhaps we should see about building an extension.'

'Maybe.' Roy lit a cigarette, ignoring Harley and Sammy's disapproving looks. Too late to stop now. He'd tried, half-heartedly, a couple of times and almost given up, but life was too stressful and he needed his fags. He didn't smoke indoors any more, so that was an improvement. He closed his eyes and thought about the birthday surprise he'd be springing on Sammy. Unbeknown to her, he'd bought back her beloved Jasmine House from the boy band she'd sold it to following their divorce. It was in the throes of a complete makeover, courtesy of their interior designer son, Jason. Roy had instructed him to spare no expense: it had to be perfect.

Sammy wasn't too happy at turning sixty soon. He thought buying their old home might soften the blow. Hopefully they'd recapture some more of the magic they'd lost. He felt happier now than he'd felt in a long time; he wanted to make sure she did too. A feeling of contentment washed over him. A feeling he was getting used to. Life was pretty sweet and about to get even better. So much to look forward to. His new grandchildren *and* the house. He finished his cigarette. 'I'll start the barbecue and —' He stopped as the telephone rang out in the kitchen. Bloody phone, always disturbing his peace. Harley struggled to her feet, announcing that she needed the loo and would pick up the call.

Roy stood up. The boys were getting noisier and a loud squeal made him jump. 'RJ, don't pull Danny's hair like that,' he shouted. 'Naughty boy. Come here, Dan.'

'Daddy,' Danny yelled as he ran to Roy, who caught hold of

him and sat back down, holding him close. He stroked his blond curls and wiped his blue eyes with a tissue. He loved the little boy as though he were his own. He looked up as Harley returned.

'It was Livvy,' she said. 'The tour's finished. She got an earlier fight from the States and she's getting the shuttle up from Heathrow. She'll pick the boys up at seven.'

'Bloody hell,' said Roy. 'That's all we need.'

'She never thinks.' Sammy tutted. 'Why can't she wait until tomorrow and we'll take them home ourselves like we arranged? I hate her coming here. Sorry, love, I know she's your real mother, but...'

'Mum, it's okay, I understand,' Harley said.

'What time is it now?' Roy asked.

'Five thirty,' Sammy said. 'Doesn't give us much time to get organised. Forget the barbecue, make them beans on toast. I'm getting in the bath. No way is she seeing me in gardening shorts and a scruffy top!'

Roy shook his head as she hurried away. Scruffy top? Sammy never looked anything but immaculate. 'I could throttle Livvy at times,' he said to Harley. 'She's a bloody nuisance, swapping arrangements without warning. She knows damn well that Sammy doesn't like her coming here.'

* * *

Sammy pulled the curtains across and lay down on the big brass bed while the bath filled. She stared up at the beamed ceiling, smiling as a little spider spun an intricate web just above the window. He'd have to go before bedtime, but for now she'd leave him in peace. She could feel a headache starting. Probably tension, she thought. Hardly surprising, with her nemesis dropping in later. She turned as Roy came into the room.

'You okay, darling? You look a bit pale.'

'I'm tired,' she said. 'And annoyed too.'

He bent to kiss her. 'I know. And I'm sorry she's messed up our last night with the boys.'

Sammy sighed. 'Go and see to their tea. I'll be down as soon as I'm ready.'

She closed her eyes, but found it impossible to switch off. A nice soak would work wonders, she hoped. There was no way she was greeting Livvy without full make-up, freshly-washed hair and figure-hugging clothes. That was one thing she still had in her favour – her slim waistline and long, slender legs. Roy was always telling her she looked wonderful for an old bird, cheeky sod that he was.

* * *

Sammy lay back in the bubbles and closed her eyes. Bliss. She could hear the boys jabbering as they came upstairs. She heard Harley chastising RJ. With his thick dark hair and big brown eyes he was the spit of Roy and Harley, but a right little devil at times.

'See you later, Mum. I'm off out soon,' Harley called. 'Sorry I can't stay until Livvy arrives, but I'd already made arrangements. Tell her I'll catch up with her tomorrow.'

'Okay, sweetheart.' She wished Harley could stay – she always managed to diffuse any tense situation when her birth mother was around.

Sammy didn't mind Roy sharing joint custody of the boys with Livvy. Even though Danny was not his flesh and blood, she and Roy had formed a bond with the little lad. He had a sweet and gentle nature. Livvy had reappeared in their lives when Harley was sixteen. Roy became re-involved and when Sammy discovered Livvy was pregnant again, she'd eventually called time on their marriage, even though it wasn't really what Roy wanted. A few months after their divorce, she realised her mistake: in spite of all the pain and betrayal, she was still in love with him and he with her. Roy begged her forgiveness and in time they remarried. This time it was for keeps, she was determined. She knew Livvy still had a hold over him with their children but there was no way she was getting her hands on him again. She climbed out of the bath and wrapped herself in a big fluffy towel, ready for a pampering session that would keep Roy's eyes glued to her, and her alone.

* * *

'Right, boys, sit on the sofa and wait quietly for Mommy,' Roy said as RJ sucked his thumb and twiddled the ear of his bunny. Danny yawned and rubbed his eyes, snuggling into the favourite old blanket he always took to bed with him.

The lounge door opened and Sammy walked in, flicking her long, light-brown hair over her shoulders. She perched on the arm of the sofa and he stood in front of her. He gazed down into cool blue eyes that held a wicked twinkle. She could still turn him on and she knew it. 'Wow! Looking good, Mrs C.' He pulled her up and into his arms, pressing against her.

He loved the way her tight black jeans sat neatly on slim hips. He ran his hands over her firm backside, clutching her closer. Her cream silk sweater, with the wide neckline, slid off one slender shoulder as he held her. He buried his face in her neck, breathing in the seductive scent of her perfume. He wished he could drag her back up the stairs right now and make love to her.

'Just a little something I threw together,' she whispered, running her hands through his hair.

'You know, Sam, for a woman clocking sixty, you look terrific. I'm so proud to be seen with you – I love you.'

'I love you, too,' she said, pulling him onto the sofa. 'But don't get any ideas before *she* arrives. It's taken me ages to get ready, you can save it for later.'

'Just one kiss to keep me going,' he said, leaning in.

'Roy!' Sammy nodded at the boys, who both had their eyes shut now. 'Oh, look, poor little things. Fast asleep already, they should be in bed.'

'Might as well have that kiss then. Promise not to mess your hair up.'

She smiled and moved into his arms.

He kissed her and squeezed her and thought about how thrilled she'd be when he told her he'd bought back Jasmine House. He couldn't wait to have long, loving nights in their old bedroom; to share the new Jacuzzi bath with her, as they'd done so many times in the past, with an accompanying bottle of wine. Here at the cottage there was no Jacuzzi and the bathroom, tucked under the thatched eaves, had such a small bath and at over six-foot tall, he was hard pushed to lay full-length in it, never mind share.

'What are you grinning at?' Sammy asked.

'Oh, you know. Just thinking about later,' he said, winking at her. He looked at the clock: it was now seven thirty. Typical of Livvy that she didn't think to call and let them know she was running late.

'Wish she'd hurry up,' Sammy said. 'I feel all churned up inside.'

'I know,' Roy said. 'Me too.' The doorbell rang. He got up to answer and let in Livvy and a tall, grey-haired, denim-clad man, wearing a Stetson and a big friendly smile. 'Come on in, the kids are asleep. Pity you couldn't leave them until tomorrow.'

Livvy shook her head, blonde curls bouncing. 'I want them home tonight. I've not seen them for four weeks. You remember Hank, my drummer.' She introduced the man to Roy.

'I do,' Roy said, shaking Hank's outstretched hand. 'How are you doing, Hank?'

'Howdy,' Hank replied. 'I'm doing good, thanks, Roy, and you?'

'Not bad, thanks.' Roy nodded. 'Come through, they're on the sofa.'

Sammy got to her feet as Livvy ran into the room and fell to her knees beside her sleeping sons. She dropped kisses on their heads and hugged them. 'I've so missed them. Have they been okay?'

'They've been fine,' Sammy said. 'You could have called more often, you know.'

Livvy shrugged. 'I don't like being a nuisance. And I get upset when I hear their voices. Anyway, I bet they haven't missed me half as much as I've missed them. They love coming here to stay.' She got to her feet and took Hank's hand. 'Hank and I have some good news to share.'

Roy stood behind Sammy and put his hands on her shoulders. 'News?'

'Yes. We, err... we got married last week in Vegas!' She held out her hand to show off a plain gold band.

'Married? Well, congratulations,' Roy said. 'I didn't even know you two were an item.'

Hank cleared his throat and put an arm around his new wife's shoulders. 'We've, err... well, as you know we've been good friends for a long time. It's now over two years since my wife passed away. I felt I was ready to move on. So did Livvy.'

'I'm really pleased for you.' Roy shook Hank's hand again and pecked Livvy on the cheek. He looked into her baby-blue eyes and felt nothing. Even looking down at her neat little figure in tight denim jeans, fringed leather jacket and cowboy boots, a mass of golden curls framing her face and tumbling to her shoulders, a look that had driven him wild a few years ago, he still felt nothing. He was also surprised to find he felt no jealousy or animosity towards Hank. He breathed a deep sigh. It was definitely over. The feeling was good. He turned to Sammy and saw relief in her eyes too. She pecked Hank on the cheek and gave Livvy a hug.

'I guess we should have a drink to toast you,' Roy said. 'Sam, there's a bottle of Moët in the fridge. Will you do the honours, love?'

Sammy nodded and smiled. 'My pleasure. Please take a seat, I won't be a minute.'

* * *

In the kitchen Sammy leant against the worktop and said a silent prayer of thanks to whomever. Livvy, married, meant there'd be less likelihood of her calling Roy so often in the future. She was constantly having him run back and forth to Ashlea Grange if one of the boys was ill, or for any excuse she could come up with. She usually called his mobile too and not the cottage landline, which always left Sammy feeling uneasy. Now she'd got Hank to rely on, life hopefully would get much better. She poured four flutes of Moët and carried the tray into the lounge.

'Well, here's to the pair of you.' Roy held up his glass in a toast. 'I hope you settle down okay at the Grange, Hank. You'll soon get used to the UK weather.'

'Thank you.' Hank cleared his throat as Livvy's cheeks flushed bright pink.

'I'll tell them, honey,' Livvy said and put her glass down on the coffee table. 'We've no plans to live at Ashlea Grange, Roy. Hank has four daughters and grandchildren in LA so we're going back to the States and taking the boys with us. It's all arranged. We'll be living there permanently from next month.'

Sammy felt Roy stiffen beside her. He gave a strangled gasp and put down his glass.

'Over my dead body!' he roared, startling RJ into wakefulness.

'You can't stop me taking them,' Livvy said as RJ began to cry. 'I knew you'd be like this. They're *my* babies.'

'They're Roy's too,' Sammy said and picked RJ up and cuddled him. He snuggled into her neck, thumb back in his mouth, eyes closed again. Sammy swallowed hard. She loved the still-baby scent of him and stroked his sweaty little head. She couldn't bear to part with him and as much as he complained about kids under his feet all the time, she knew it would destroy Roy to lose them both.

'There's no way you're taking them to the States. If you want to go off with Hank, that's fine, but the boys stay here,' Roy said, quieter this time.

'We'll see about that,' Livvy snapped. She took RJ from Sammy. 'Hank, you carry Danny out to the car.'

'I hope you've got some child seats in the car,' Roy said, standing by the lounge door as Livvy tried to push past him.

'Of course we have. We went home to get my car and they were already in there. I'm not that stupid, you know.'

'Honey,' Hank said, lifting Danny up, 'just go get in the car. We'll discuss this tomorrow with Roy.'

'Nothing to discuss,' Roy said. 'They stay in the UK with me and Sammy. And not only that,' he directed at Livvy, 'our daughter is due to give birth to your first grandchildren soon. Don't you even care enough to wait?'

'I'll be back for the birth,' she said. 'Hank will take care of the boys, they'll be fine with him. Two of his girls are mothers, they'll help look after them for however long I'm over here.'

'You haven't a bloody clue about parenting!' Roy shook his head. 'You dumped Harley on me and Sam, and now you're talking of taking the boys to another country and leaving them with strangers? No disrespect to Hank, but what about when you're both on tour, or recording for weeks at a time? Who'll look after them then? I'm sorry, Livvy, but I'll fight you to the ends of the earth for custody. They're going nowhere.'

2

Livvy tucked RJ back into bed and smoothed his hair off his forehead. His cheeks were flushed, long lashes still damp, but at least he was peaceful now after crying out for Sammy and Daddy. Coming home always unsettled him for a few days. She crept out of the nursery and crossed the landing to her bedroom. Hank stretched out on the bed, snoring softly, not even disturbed by the screams of a toddler. No surprise though, seeing as it was 4:00 a.m. and he'd hardly slept for forty-eight hours. The tour had been exhausting, as always. She'd missed her boys and Harley, and Courtney, her daughter from her first marriage, away on a world trip with her partner, Jamie. She'd been hoping to come back to word from her, but there wasn't so much as a postcard.

In the en suite she took two paracetamol, washed them down with a glass of water and pressed her forehead against the wall. The cool marble did nothing for her pounding head. She'd need to call her lawyer tomorrow. No way was she giving her sons to Roy and Sammy. They'd agreed from the start to share custody and so far it had worked just fine. Her tours were shorter now, none of the big stadiums she'd played years ago. At least she knew the boys were well looked after when she was out of the country. Part of the agreement had been that she and Roy made sure they weren't touring at the same time. Surely, once he got used to the idea, he'd see that now she and Hank were married, the boys would be better off with *them*.

Back in bed, she lay stiffly beside Hank, who grunted and rolled over, flinging his arm across her middle. He nuzzled her ear and brushed his hand over her stomach and down between her thighs but she pushed it away, whispering that she was too tired. They'd already made love tonight and she really couldn't be bothered right now. She heard him sigh and he turned back onto his left side. Within minutes he was snoring again. He was twenty-two years older than her and two years older than Roy. He made her feel safe but she wasn't in love with him. They'd been friends since she'd joined his band Juice many years ago. He'd always looked out for her, taking her side with the inevitable squabbles between band members. He'd been devastated when his wife, whom he'd married in his teens, passed away and now it was *her* turn to look after *him*.

They'd grown closer after last year's Grand Ole Opry and had kept in daily contact. She'd visited him in LA a few months later. Her unwritten rule, that she never got romantically involved with any member of the band, had gone out the window when she and Hank became lovers. He asked her to marry him at the start of the new tour and she couldn't think of any reason to say no. She knew she'd never replace his wife, and for her, Roy would always be her one true love. But being with Hank would give her and the boys stability and help combat the loneliness she felt when she wasn't touring. And now Roy, who claimed to have everything he wanted, or so he told her, threatened to screw up her plans for a happy future – again. Well, not if *she* had anything to do with it. He'd messed her around just once too often.

* * *

'Oh wow, look at the size of you!' Livvy flung her arms around Harley. 'Come on outside and say hi to Hank.' She led the way into the kitchen and out through the French windows, where RJ, Danny and Hank were having breakfast on the patio. 'You remember my daughter, Harley?' she said to Hank.

'I sure do.' Hank rose to his feet. 'Have a seat. Would you like breakfast? I made pancakes.'

'Yes, please.' Harley sat down at the picnic table as Livvy followed Hank inside.

'Harley,' RJ said, 'we going seaside soon with Momma and Yank.'

'Hank, not Yank,' Harley said, smiling at her little brother. 'That should be fun. You can go on the rides. Danny will love that, won't you?'

Danny nodded. 'You come too, Harley?'

'We'll see, sweetie. I have lots to do this week.'

Livvy carried out a jug of fresh orange juice and a dish of pancakes and Harley helped herself.

'Mmm, a proper American breakfast.' She drizzled the pancakes with maple syrup. 'Love them but I only ever get them when you're home, Mom. Dad tried to make them but they stuck to the griddle.'

Livvy smiled. Roy had always been useless in the kitchen.

'Is it okay if me and Jack move back in later?' Harley continued. 'And will you help me plan the nursery? I'll use the little spare room for the first few months. We can't stay at Mum and Dad's when the babies arrive. But you're home now for a few months, aren't you? I'd really like you around when I give birth.'

Livvy chewed her lip. Harley was so excited. *She* was too. Being a grandma was a very special privilege and she was looking forward to it. She looked up as Hank called from the kitchen.

'Doorbell, honey. Shall I get it?'

'Please.' She turned her attention back to Harley, who was looking at her quizzically, no doubt wondering why Hank was here. 'Of course you can move back in. You could have stayed here while we were away. You didn't have to camp out at your dad and Sammy's.'

'I find this place spooky when you're not around,' Harley said. 'It's too big and it creaks.'

'That's because she's a real old lady of a house.' Livvy sighed. She'd be sad to leave Ashlea Grange. Roy had bought the old Tudor-style mansion as their marital home but the marriage never happened and he moved out. Harley and Jack moved in on their wedding day, which should also have been *her* wedding day. She shook her head; best not to dwell on it. She should hate Roy Cantello for screwing up her life, but she couldn't and he'd given her beautiful children in Harley and RJ. She was distracted by a noise at the French windows and looked up to see her other daughter Courtney beaming, Hank smiling over her shoulder.

'Sweetie, how good to see you!' Livvy leapt to her feet and flung her arms around her girl. 'Jamie not with you?'

'The cab driver dropped him at his place,' Courtney said. 'He had to go see his mom. It's her birthday. He'll be over later. Oh my God!' she shrieked as Harley struggled to her feet. 'Wow, that's some bump, sis.'

Livvy looked on as her daughters embraced, both talking at once. They were so alike, except for their colouring. Harley, as dark as her half-Italian father, while blue-eyed Courtney's blonde curls tumbled over her shoulders. Both had heart-shaped faces and the same mannerisms, just like hers.

'So come on, sit down and tell us about your trip,' Livvy said. 'I've been concerned that there's been no contact from you for a while.'

'I couldn't get hold of you, Mom. I did try last week but

your phone wouldn't take calls and your message service wasn't working. I spoke to Harley, so I knew when you were due home and timed it to surprise you.'

'We got back a day early,' Livvy said, feeling her face warming. She'd turned her phone off the day she and Hank got married and left it off for the following twenty-four hours. She looked down at her hands in her lap. She'd sneakily slipped off her new wedding ring and shoved it in her pocket when Harley arrived. It could stay there until she'd told her daughters her news – well, about the marriage anyway. Telling them she was moving to the States and taking the boys could wait until she'd spoken to her lawyer. 'Come indoors for a few minutes, I've something to tell you both.' She raised an eyebrow in Hank's direction. 'You okay to stay out here with the boys, Hank?'

'Sure, go ahead. We'll have a game of soccer. Find your ball, boys.' He lifted RJ down and wiped his sticky chin. Danny scrambled down after him and they shot off across the lawn towards the little white-painted goal posts, giggling with excitement.

'You sure you can keep up with them?' Harley said. 'They run Dad ragged.'

'I'll do my best,' Hank said and set off up the garden.

'Go and sit in the lounge, girls, and I'll bring coffee through,' Livvy said. She stared after them as they left the kitchen. Her stomach churned, she felt nervous and needed a few minutes to compose herself.

* * *

'It's so good to see you again, Courtney.' Harley flopped onto one of the sofas and put her feet up on a nearby footstool. Courtney sat down next to her. 'I've missed you so much, missed Mom too. Be great to have everyone together again.'

'It will,' Courtney agreed. 'How long now?' She gently rubbed Harley's wriggling bump.

'Ten weeks. Unless they come a bit early, of course. Can't wait. I'm so uncomfortable and they're never still. Jack's really excited. It's one of each, by the way.'

'Oooh, my little nephew and niece,' Courtney said, hugging Harley. 'How lovely! I was praying you wouldn't go into labour until we got home. The family's going to be huge! Good job Mom's got this big house.' She lowered her voice. 'How come her drummer's here? Have you seen the way he looks at her, as though they're, erm, together? I know they're good friends, but he doesn't usually come back to the UK with her when a tour ends.'

'Don't know.' Harley shrugged. 'I wondered the same. They do look a bit love-struck. Well, *he* does anyway. I was gonna say he's too old for her and then thought better not – he's a similar age to Dad.' She stopped as her mother came in carrying a tray, eyebrows raised questioningly.

'Problem?' Livvy asked, putting the tray on the coffee table and settling down on the opposite sofa.

'No, Mom,' Harley said. 'Just wondered about Hank being here, that's all. You look a bit, err... comfortable together.' She saw Courtney's raised eyebrows and suppressed a grin.

Livvy nodded. 'Hank and I got married last week – in Vegas.'

Both girls stared, mouths open.

Livvy half-smiled. 'Well, aren't you going to congratulate me?'

'Married? To Hank!' Harley exclaimed. 'I wasn't expecting that.'

'Nor me.' Courtney shook her head. 'But hey, Mom, if he makes you happy, then yeah, congratulations.' She hoisted Harley to her feet and Livvy jumped up and joined them in a group hug.

'Do you love him?' Harley asked as they sat back down. 'You know, I mean, *really* love him – like you loved Dad?'

'Roy will always be special to me,' Livvy said, her eyes filling with sudden tears, 'but I'm not the one for him. It's time to move on. Hank loves me and I kind of love him. It's different, but he makes me feel happy and safe. I'm sure we can make it work.'

Harley frowned, unconvinced. Mom wasn't meeting her eye and those tears bothered her. And happy – safe? Was that enough to build a future on? Her mom was still young at forty-two. And that 'kind of' loving him comment was odd for a newlywed. She thought about Dad and her mum, Sammy. They were always hugging and laughing and he was forever whispering in Mum's ear so that she blushed and smacked his arm. She hoped she and Jack would still be into one another like that when *they* were really old. She turned her attention back to Mom: 'So, how will Hank take to living in the UK? What about his family? Will they be coming here too?'

Livvy shook her head. 'His daughters are married with their own families, they all live in LA.'

'Won't he miss them?' Courtney asked.

'I'm sure he will. But hey, we can visit and they can come and stay with us.' She jumped to her feet. 'I need to make an urgent phone call. I'll do it from my room. Why don't you two go back outside and see if those little rascals have finished Hank off?'

* * *

Livvy sat on the bed, hugging the phone. She'd made an appointment to see her lawyer at four. What was the betting Roy had already seen his? She opened her bedside cupboard and reached for the box where she kept her family papers. She took out RJ's and Danny's birth certificates. Roy was registered as father on both. How she wished now that she'd had her late husband's name on Daniel's but Roy had insisted that Daniel should have his surname and had registered the birth while she was recovering in hospital. It was too late now to do anything about that. She rooted further. Damn, the boys' passports weren't here. Roy must still have them from when he and Sammy took them to Disneyland, Paris, at Easter. If she asked for them back now, she knew he would refuse. She could ask Harley to get them, but then Harley would wonder why she couldn't ask Roy direct and she'd be bound to say something to him anyway.

She jumped as the phone rang out and looked at the caller display. Talk of the devil – well, think of him anyway! 'Hello, Roy.' She held the phone away from her ear as he launched into a tirade. When he'd finished, she spoke as calmly as she could: 'Fine. I'm seeing mine later today, I'll speak to you tonight.' She was silent as she listened to him again. 'Yes, well no matter what your guy says, Danny is *my* child, not yours. I can take him wherever I want to. I'll fight you for RJ, and believe me, I'll win. A child is always better off living with its mother.' She tried hard to hold back the tears as he reminded her that she didn't think that when she left Harley with him. 'I'm not arguing with you, Roy. I'm going now. The girls are here and I need to spend time with them. And no, I haven't told them yet. And I'd appreciate it if you didn't say anything to Harley later. She knows Hank and I are married, but that's all for now.'

She said goodbye and hung up. God, he sounded angry. And that dig about leaving Harley was uncalled for. It had been the most painful thing she'd ever had to do. Something she'd regretted all her life since. But she felt her daughter should know her father and that was impossible unless she gave him full care and control. He wasn't prepared to marry her, he wanted to stay married to Sammy. She couldn't bear to be in the same town and see them playing happy families with her baby,

so she'd made her choice and moved on. Except she never had –
moved on, that is – in spite of her marriage to Courtney and
Danny's late father, Daniel. She'd been in love with Roy since
the very first kiss and probably always would be.

In the bathroom she splashed her face with cold water,
forced a happy, newlywed smile and went back downstairs,
wondering how the hell she could get her boys' passports back.

3

Roy sped up the drive of Jasmine House, wheels spinning, gravel flying. He winced as loose stones hit the bonnet of his new BMW saloon, heart lifting slightly at the sight of his beloved old family home. He'd purchased the run-down Edwardian house and land for peanuts in 1966 when The Raiders were starting to make it big. Sammy's design skills had soon transformed the place into their dream home. The thrill at the thought of returning with her was quickly replaced by a rush of sadness and memories of happier times when they'd lived here with their sons, Nick and Jason.

Roy dashed his hand across his eyes, his mind in a whirl. Livvy had seemed almost unconcerned when he'd called her earlier, as though certain she had all the rights. But she was taking his little lads nowhere. The solicitor told him she couldn't without his permission anyway and no way was he giving it. Knowing her, she'd try and stop his access altogether. Well, as far as he was concerned, she could piss off back to the States with Hank as soon as she liked, minus the boys. He pulled up in front of the garage block and blasted his horn. Jason appeared and waved from the doorstep. Roy smiled and waved back. Tall, slim and dark, Jason was the image of himself in his thirties, before the silver overtook the black. Still, Sammy liked it; called him her silver fox. Roy leapt out of the car and they made their way inside.

'Good to see you, son. You're looking well.'

'You too, Dad. Why the suit?' Jason gave him a hug and led him through to the spacious kitchen, overlooking the back garden. A pot of coffee bubbled on the new hob. He poured two mugs. 'Black?'

'Please.' Roy took the mug. 'Been to the solicitor's, hence the suit. Looks great in here,' he said, changing the subject. 'Didn't we have white units and black granite worktops before though?' He pulled a packet of cigarettes from his jacket pocket.

'You did. Mum loved them so I've chosen similar, but updated the units and tiles.' Jason frowned as Roy took out his lighter. 'Not in here, Dad. Light up on the patio. Start as you mean to go on – a smoke-free zone for Harley's new babies.'

Roy rolled his eyes, but stepped outside and lit up. He pointed to the newly landscaped plot where the swimming pool used to be. 'They've done a good job, Jase.' The pool area, filled in now, was freshly turfed, with roses at the far end, bordered by low-growing lavender bushes: Sammy's favourites. 'Glad that's gone. I'm too old to be diving in and rescuing kids.' He laughed. 'Nobody used it anyway and the heating and mainte-nance bills were through the roof.'

Jason nodded. 'Shame we didn't have it when Nick was around. He loved to swim.' He fell silent for a moment and Roy saw a faraway look in his dark-brown eyes.

'You still miss your brother, don't you?' He placed a hand on Jason's shoulder.

Jason wiped a lone tear. 'Twenty-one years nearly and I miss him like crazy.'

Roy sighed. 'So do me and Mum,' he said, a catch in his voice. 'I wish I could relive 1984 and wipe out everything bad.'

His affair with Livvy and the loss of his eldest son in a car crash that year weighed heavily on his shoulders.

'But then you wouldn't have Harley, Dad. You love her to bits, *and* little Roy.'

'I know.' Roy stared out across the gardens at Alderley Edge in the distance and the surrounding rolling countryside. He took a long drag on his cigarette, exhaling slowly. 'Livvy got married last week to her drummer. She wants to take my boys to live in LA permanently.'

Jason's jaw dropped. 'Married? Bloody hell! How does that make you feel?'

Roy shrugged. 'I'm glad that she's found someone, hope it works out for them. But she's not having my kids.'

Jason stared. 'Can you stop her though? I mean, you're not Danny's father. Surely she has more rights?'

'I'm registered as his father. Christ, let's face it, son, right up to the birth I thought I was his father and so did she. He's been brought up as mine. I couldn't part with him any more than I can let Roy Junior go. The solicitor said she can't take them without my consent anyway. I told him I'm after sole custody. Livvy's got a fight on her hands.'

'How does Mum feel? About sole custody, I mean? It'll be hard work on a permanent basis and you're not getting any younger.' Jason shook his head. 'I find Daisy a handful,' he said, referring to his four-year old daughter. 'Jules would like another but *I'm* not up for it.' Jason and his partner Jules had had Daisy by surrogate, Jason being the sperm donor.

Roy smiled. His little granddaughter was a delight. The worries he'd had about Jason and Jules becoming parents had flown out the window when he saw how competently the two had taken to the role. And Daisy was totally unfazed by the fact that she had two daddies. 'She's a handful alright, takes after her Auntie Harley. God help you, Jase! Your Mum's okay about us having the boys full-time, it'd break her heart to lose them. We'll get some help in. She's more concerned about lack of space at the cottage and she's talking about getting an extension built. I'm going to suggest she lets Harley and Jack have the cottage when we move in here. They're ready for their own place. It'll be a great first home for them and the twins.'

'What about Ashlea Grange? Will you sell it when Livvy goes away?'

Roy took a last drag on his ciggie. 'Yep. The Grange is in my name. It'll free up some capital. Right, let's take a wander around. Show me what you've been up to. Did you get the Jacuzzi sorted for our en suite?'

* * *

'Sam?' Roy called, letting himself into the cottage.

'Up here,' she called back.

He slung his jacket over the newel post and ran up the stairs. Sammy was seated in front of the dressing table, brushing her hair. She smiled at his reflection.

'How did it go? You were ages.'

'Popped into Flanagan and Grey's to see Jon and Sean,' he fibbed and hoped his face wouldn't give anything away. From the tour Jason gave him, Jasmine House looked perfect so far and should be complete by the end of next week. He was going to suggest a romantic weekend away and take her home instead. He could feel his face cracking with a grin and tried to suppress it. 'It went well. Our solicitor says she can't take them abroad without my consent. He's applying to the courts for sole custody. She'll be instructing her solicitor to do the same, so I expect it to drag on for quite a while. She'll have to go without them if she wants to be with Hank.'

'Good. We can't lose them,' she said, her eyes filling with tears.

Roy went to the wardrobe and lifted down a briefcase. He

rooted inside and pulled out two passports: 'Just making sure we've got these. Whatever you do, don't give them back to her. I promise you, we won't lose the kids.' He pulled her to her feet and into his arms. Her silky robe parted and slithered to the floor, pooling around their feet. She was naked underneath. He felt the blood rush to his groin. 'Sam, I love you so much,' he said, lowering her onto the bed.

'I love you too, but Ed and Jane are expecting us for lunch,' she whispered as he dropped little kisses on her face and neck.

'They won't mind us being a bit late.' He kissed her long and hard, running his fingers through her hair.

'Have to be a quickie then!' She kissed him back.

He smiled, loving the way she responded. Sammy had always been a great lover, right from their first time. Lying here with her now he couldn't imagine why on earth he'd ever cheated on her. She was everything – his world.

* * *

Roy passed Eddie a cigarette as they took a seat at the picnic table in Eddie's large, rambling garden. Sammy had gone inside to help Jane carry out the food *and*, Roy suspected, to have a grumble about Livvy's plans.

'So, what've you been up to since the weekend?' Eddie asked, holding out his lighter.

'Not a lot. Livvy took the kids home. You know about her plans, 'cos Sam spoke to Jane. I saw my solicitor earlier.' He lowered his voice. 'I popped into Jasmine House too. It's nearly ready.'

'Great. She still has no idea?'

'Not a clue. Can't wait to see her face when...' He stopped as Jane, carrying a tray, led the way outside, Sammy following with a carafe of red wine.

'Pizza, salad and warm olive bread,' Jane announced, setting the tray down on the table. 'Isn't it nice to be able to eat outside? Better make the most of it though because it's forecast rain again for next week.'

'It's being so bloody cheerful that keeps you going, Jane,' Eddie said, winking at her.

'Cheeky!' She smacked his hand. 'Right, just help yourselves. Ed, pour the wine, please.'

Eddie filled their glasses. 'Got a new song on the go,' he said, turning to Roy. 'We'll go up to the music room later, see what you think.'

'Great, I feel ready for a bit of creativity.' Roy took a swig of wine. 'We need to get our heads into gear for the next album and the autumn tour.'

'How's Harley?' Jane asked. 'I can't wait for the babies. Great-grandma, can you believe it! I'm so excited and Jess is beside herself.' Harley was married to Jane and Eddie's student grandson Jack, the son of their daughter, Jessica. 'We really will be related by blood then.'

Roy laughed. 'So what does that make you, Ed and me, Jane?'

She smiled. 'Not a clue, Roy, but we'll be linked somehow.'

Roy felt himself relaxing and finished his wine. He tried to push thoughts of Livvy and his kids to the back of his mind and tucked into his lunch. Eddie topped up his glass and he took another swig. There was something to be said for being older, not quite retired, but older all the same. Life was more leisurely, when the boys weren't around, that was. He looked at Sammy and Jane, talking animatedly about the expected twins and how it would be lovely to enjoy the grandchildren, knowing they could hand them back when they'd had enough. Was he being fair to Sammy in expecting her to bring up his boys when she should be taking life more easily? Still, she loved them and said she didn't want to lose them. But would full-time be too much? And what about touring? How would she manage on her own?

DREAMS ON MERSEY SQUARE

They'd have to employ a live-in nanny. Jasmine House would be overrun instead of the peaceful haven he'd planned for Sammy. Damn Livvy for screwing up his nice, serene future.

'That's yours, Roy,' Sammy said as an explosion of music blasted from his jacket pocket.

He rooted for his phone and stared at the screen: 'Livvy.' He frowned. 'Hello.' He got up and paced around the patio. 'Be there as soon as I can.' He ended the call and saw Sammy looking anxiously at him.

'What is it? Why does she want you to go over?'

'Harley doesn't feel too well. Livvy's going to her lawyer appointment. She hasn't enough time to drive over here and Hank's looking after the kids. Won't take me long and I'll bring her back here.'

'What on earth's wrong with her?' Sammy asked. 'She was fine this morning when she left us.'

'Livvy said she feels dizzy and she's got a banging headache. She doesn't think she should drive although Harley was insisting she'd be okay.' He bent to drop a kiss on Sammy's lips. 'She's been trying to contact Jack but he's probably in a lecture with his phone turned off. See if you can get hold of him and let him know. Won't be long.'

4

At the sound of crunching gravel, Livvy looked out of her bedroom window and watched as Roy pulled up outside the garage block. She turned to the bed and stroked Harley's hair from her face.

'Your dad's here now, I'll go and let him in.' She tottered down the stairs on high heels, smoothed her black pencil skirt over her hips and checked her appearance in the full-length mirror near the front door. Dressed formally for the visit to her lawyer, her hair fastened up in a neat French pleat, she looked more secretary than country rock star, but the killer heels and shiny stockings added a feminine touch. She undid the top two buttons on her white shirt, revealing her cleavage. As the bell rang, she thought better of it and fastened one up again. Roy wouldn't give her a second glance anyway. He'd be worried about Harley for one thing and would no doubt moan at her for ruining the parquet flooring with stilettos. Her stomach churned, as it always did when she was about to see him. She swallowed hard and opened the door. He had an anxious expression in his eyes and her heart thudded as he rushed in without being asked.

'Where is she?'

'Upstairs.' She led the way and stood back as he dropped to his knees beside the bed.

'How are you feeling, princess?' He took Harley's hand and kissed it.

'A bit strange. I felt all fuzzy in my head, like I was going to pass out. Mom suggested I lie down for a while, but my head's banging now and it's all at the front.'

'I've given her paracetamol,' Livvy said, 'but they don't seem to have helped. I wonder if it's high blood pressure. Did they say anything at the clinic when you got checked over yesterday?'

'No. My blood pressure was slightly high, but they didn't seem concerned; just told me to get plenty of rest. And that's all I've been doing, apart from shopping for the babies. I sit with my feet up most of the time.'

'Perhaps you've had too much sun,' Roy said. 'Anyway, come on, let's get you back to Ed's place. Mum and Jane are trying to contact Jack.'

'We're supposed to be moving back in here today when Jack gets home. My things are at your house, I need to pick them up.'

'We'll sort that out later.' Roy helped her to her feet. 'That bump looks bigger than ever. You sure you're not carrying baby elephants?'

'Dad! Just hold on to me while we go down the stairs.'

Roy and Livvy grabbed her arms as she stumbled and sat her back down on the bed.

'Right, lady, I'm taking you straight to the doctor's,' Roy said.

Livvy looked at her watch: 'I need to leave, I'll be late for my appointment. Maybe I should cancel and come with you.'

'No need,' Roy said sharply. 'I'll see to Harley, don't let us spoil your plans. Just help me get her to the car, please.'

Livvy raised a warning eyebrow. She didn't want Harley getting wind of the fact that she was seeing her lawyer. She picked up her daughter's sandals and bent to put them on her feet: 'Your ankles are swollen, sweetie. The sooner you see the doctor, the better.'

'What do you think's wrong with her?' Roy asked, his anxious expression deepening.

'Not sure,' Livvy said, frightened to meet his eyes in case she saw her fears mirrored in them. What if being pregnant had triggered something? Harley had been diagnosed with Acute Lymphoblastic Leukaemia (ALL) at the age of sixteen. A bone marrow transplant from RJ had saved her life. During the chemotherapy treatment, and at Harley's request, eggs had been harvested from her ovaries. Both she and Roy had tried to talk Harley into waiting a few years before going down the IVF route but Harley was determined to try and start their family in Jack's last year at uni. Although against Roy's better judgement, his financial status had meant there was no NHS waiting list to consider and the result was the expected twins.

Livvy sighed now as Roy grabbed her arm: 'A private word.' He led her out on to the landing. 'You think it's something serious, I can see it in your face.'

'No!' she whispered and pulled the bedroom door shut. There was no way she was voicing her concerns to him. He'd only flap and put the fear of God into Harley. 'I'm sure it's because she's not resting as much as she says she is. She admits she's been rushing around looking for things for the nursery this week. You and Sammy should make certain that she always has someone with her.'

'She does, most of the time. Don't tell me how to look after my daughter, Livvy. I brought her up, remember! Harley likes to go off and do her own thing with her mates. We had the little ones to see to as well – we couldn't cart them all around Manchester on a whim.'

'So how do you reckon you'd cope if you had full custody of the boys? It's too much to expect Sammy to take on a full-time mother role at her age. You're not being fair to her, me or the kids. And another thing...' She lowered her voice further. 'You'll have to take in Harley, Jack and the babies when I go. Either that or buy them somewhere to live. No doubt you'll sell this place.'

'That's my business and we'll all be fine,' he snapped. 'We're solid, me and Sam. We don't need you, we'll cope.'

She looked at his hand, still holding on to her upper arm and shook herself free. 'Why do you hate me so much, Roy? All I ever did was fall in love with you.'

He looked taken aback and stared at her: 'I don't hate you. I find it difficult to be civil at the moment because of your plans – I can't lose my kids.'

'Nor can I. But I can't bear to stay in this country, knowing you're only a couple of miles down the road in your love nest with Sammy. I've got the chance to be happy with Hank. Did you expect me to stay on my own forever?' She felt angry tears begin and dashed them away.

'No, I didn't. But I can't understand why Hank doesn't move to the UK.'

'His family, for one thing, and our band. It will save me having to keep flying out there for recording and shows. Anyway, arguing is getting us nowhere and I have to go. Let's get Harley out to the car.'

Roy pulled up outside Hanover's Lodge. Harley had insisted on coming there and waiting for Jack rather than be taken straight to the doctor. Sammy came running over as he turned off the engine. She yanked open the passenger door and peered in.

'She needs to see a doctor,' Roy said. 'Her feet are swollen, she's dizzy and she's got a banging head but she won't let me take her anywhere until she's spoken to Jack.'

'Jack's on his way,' Sammy said. 'Come on, love.' She helped Harley out of the car and Jane took her other arm. Between them, they took her indoors.

Roy left them to it and went to rejoin Eddie. 'She's not too clever,' he told him. 'Livvy's worried me to death. I think she feels something's going on again with the leukaemia.'

'Can't be, Harley was given the all clear after the transplant,' Eddie said.

'But what if the pregnancy *has* triggered something? Is that possible? Christ, I couldn't bear for her to go through that again, Ed. And what about the babies?'

'I'm sure they'll all be fine. Just try and relax while the girls get her sorted. Here's Jess now so they've enough hands on deck. Hiya, love,' he greeted his daughter. 'They've taken Harley indoors.'

'Thanks, Dad.'

Jess dashed inside and Eddie gave Roy a cigarette.

* * *

'We'll pop you in Jane's guest room,' Sammy said. 'It's nice and cool in there. Jess will be here in a minute, she'll have spotted your dad's car.'

'What do you think's wrong with me, Mum?' Harley said tearfully. 'My head hurts so much. Will my babies be okay? They're still wriggling around.'

'They'll be fine,' Sammy reassured her, feeling sick inside. 'Jane will call the doctor and get him to come out here to see you.'

'I'll call him now.' Jane left the room and was quickly replaced by Jess, who sat down on the bed. She took Harley's hand.

'How's my grandbabies?' Jess said, rubbing Harley's tummy gently.

'They're okay, Jess. I'm just having an off day,' Harley said as Sammy removed her sandals.

'Your feet are very puffy, sweetheart.' Sammy ran her fingers over the indents in the swollen flesh left by the cross-over straps. 'Have they been like this all day?'

Harley shook her head. 'They seemed okay this morning when I left your place. The headache and that swelling started after I felt all fuzzy.'

Jane came back in the room. 'Doc will be here as soon as he's finished his surgery. Jack's outside, your dad's telling him what's happened. I'll go and make us some tea and send him up,' she said as Harley smiled. 'I thought that would cheer you up a bit.'

'Are you okay to sit with her for a minute, Jess?' Sammy asked as footsteps pounded on the stairs and Jack rushed into the room, his blue eyes anxious, dark curls standing on end. 'Ah, no need, we can all go down and leave her in Jack's capable hands.'

* * *

Sammy sat down at the kitchen table next to Jess. Jane handed them mugs of tea. 'I don't like the look of those feet,' Sammy began.

'Nor I,' Jane agreed. 'I bet the doctor sends her straight into hospital. I think she's got pre-eclampsia. If so, they might want to deliver the babies right away.'

'Oh my God!' Jess burst into tears. 'It's far too soon, she's only thirty weeks.'

'Jess, they'll be fine. They're safer out than left in the womb. They've a great chance of survival at thirty weeks.' Jane put her arms around her daughter and held her tight. 'You had the boys early and they were okay.' Jess's twin sons had arrived at thirty-five weeks. 'Look at the size of Jack, he towers above your dad.'

Jess nodded and looked at Sammy: 'You okay, Sam?'

Sammy sighed and shook her head. 'Does anything ever go right?'

* * *

Roy felt sick. His head whirled, his thoughts all over the place. The doctor had arrived, along with Harley's community midwife, who'd been taking clinic at the surgery. Now he and Sammy were sitting in the family area at the maternity hospital while Jack had accompanied Harley to a private room, where she was awaiting the obstetrician. It looked likely that the babies would be born by caesarean section within the next twenty-four hours. The pre-eclampsia had come on suddenly and without warning. It happens, the doctor told him, when Roy had questioned why it wasn't picked up the previous day at Harley's antenatal appointment and why they weren't monitoring her more carefully considering her past medical condition.

Roy's phone vibrated against his leg in his jeans pocket. He'd switched to silent when they arrived. He looked at the screen: 'Livvy. Shall I reject the call?'

'You'd better take it,' Sammy said. 'She'll be worrying.'

'I can't do with talking to her right now.'

'Roy, you don't have a choice. Harley's her daughter.'

He pressed answer, let Livvy ramble on for a minute and then interrupted her flow: 'We're at the hospital. Harley's got pre-eclampsia, looks like the babies will be delivered soon. Well yeah, of course. See you later then.' He snapped the phone shut. 'She's coming over with Courtney.'

'What about the boys?'

'She'll leave them with Hank, they're already in bed.'

Sammy nodded. 'You should call Jason, let him know what's happening.'

'I rang him earlier while you were indoors at Ed's. I'll bring him up to date. I'm nipping outside for a fag, love. My nerves are shot.'

'Well, don't come back in stinking of smoke and use that stuff near the door to clean your hands.'

* * *

Sammy picked up a magazine from the table under the window. She flicked through the pages but couldn't concentrate. A feeling of deep panic settled within her. A here-we-go-again feeling. Livvy, babies, family conflict... it was never-ending. The sixteen years of peace when Livvy walked away seemed a lifetime ago. The four years since she'd been back had been nothing short of chaotic: Harley's illness, their divorce, Livvy's first husband's death, the births of Danny and RJ and then Sammy and Roy's remarriage. It was a time in their lives when they should be taking things much easier. Ah well, they'd cope. They hadn't got much choice and the main thing now was worrying about the health of Harley and her twins. Roy swore he wouldn't get involved with Livvy again and she had to have faith but her trust in him had been dented and would take many years to rebuild. Their love was strong, she couldn't deny that, but Livvy would always be in their lives and there was no getting away from it.

She looked up as the door opened and Jack came in. Her heart went out to him. He had a little-boy-lost look, eyes red-rimmed. He and Harley had dated since their mid-teens and were coming up to their third wedding anniversary. She sent a silent prayer to a God she wasn't sure she believed in to let things be okay for the little family.

'What's happening, Jack?' She patted the seat beside her.

'They're trying to stabilise her blood pressure with steroids,' Jack said, his voice husky with tears. 'It'll help the babies too, they said, their lungs and stuff. They're gonna deliver them in the morning after she's been on the steroids for about twelve hours.' He sat down and looked at Sammy: 'I'll be a daddy by this time tomorrow.'

'Oh, Jack.' Sammy hugged him close. 'Have you called your mum and dad?'

He nodded. 'Where's Roy?'

'Outside, having a ciggie. Livvy and Courtney are on the way. Will you be allowed in theatre while they deliver the babies?'

'Yes. I've been told I have to sit at the top end with Harley. She'll be awake so we get to see the babies as they come out. I'm terrified, but excited as well. I just hope Harley will be okay and this thing she's got goes away once the babies are here.'

'It will,' Sammy said, feigning a confidence she didn't completely feel. 'Ah, here's Roy now.'

Roy strolled in, followed by Livvy and Courtney. Sammy's stomach tightened as she looked at Livvy, her hair and make-up immaculate. She and Courtney could pass as sisters. No way did she look old enough to be almost a grandma. She glanced at Roy but could see nothing in his eyes to worry her, nothing except anxiety for his daughter.

'Jack, everything okay?' Roy asked.

Jack told them what was happening before adding, 'I guess there's no point in you all staying here overnight. I'll call you if there's anything to report. They said I can stay with her – I'll sleep in the chair by the bed. As soon as I'm told what's happening tomorrow, I'll let you know.'

'Okay, Jack,' Roy said. 'We should all go home, try and get some sleep.' He sighed heavily as Livvy's eyes filled with tears. 'She'll be fine, Liv. She's a fighter, that girl of ours.'

Sammy swallowed hard and looked at him. He grabbed her hand as though realising what he'd said and squeezed it. 'And ours,' he added quietly.

5

Roy lay on his back and stared at the ceiling. He and Sammy had come up to bed as soon as they arrived home, both drained after the day's events, but sleep evaded him. He'd tossed and turned for hours, disturbing Sammy, who told him to go to the spare room as she was knackered and they'd need to be fresh for tomorrow. The little guest room under the thatch was airless, even with the window open. There was no happy medium with this place, it was either freezing or roasting. He got up for a pee, went downstairs and opened the French door in the kitchen.

He brewed a mug of Sammy's chamomile tea, pointless making his usual black coffee; he'd be wired to the eyeballs. He sat at the table, staring out across the dark garden, lit a cigarette and wondered how Harley was getting on. Had the steroids done their job yet? He was dreading tomorrow but if bringing the babies early would save their lives *and* Harley's, then it had to be done. How he wished she'd listened to him and waited. At just over twenty, he felt she and Jack were too young to be bringing up a family. After everything she'd been through, her fight against leukaemia and the stem cell transplant from RJ, they should have waited a few more years. They could have been going off around the world and having fun before settling down but Harley had always been a headstrong little madam and his advice had fallen on deaf ears.

Sammy said she was just like him and when had *he* ever listened to his parents? She was right, of course – Harley was a definite chip off the old Cantello block. He wondered how Livvy had got on at the lawyer's. She hadn't mentioned it at the hospital, but then it was hardly the time or the place and Courtney had been with her. He'd have to wait until he could get her alone to talk. He finished his cigarette and tipped the last of the tea down the sink. How Sammy could drink gallons of that crap, he didn't know, but she insisted it helped her stay calm and relaxed. He closed the French door and took himself slowly back upstairs. He wondered fleetingly if he should climb back into bed with Sammy to help him chill. He peeped into the bedroom: she was flat out. Dare he wake her? Shaking his head, he went back into the spare room. Early morning was the best time to disturb her if he didn't want his head bitten off. She was usually obliging and in a good mood first thing. He lay on his back and willed sleep to come.

* * *

Livvy crept past the nursery door, avoiding the creaky floorboard, and hurried silently downstairs. She couldn't sleep, there was so much stuff hurtling around her head. Her lawyer had said pretty much the same as Roy's: she'd need Roy's permission to take the boys out of the country. She'd had words with Hank earlier and felt angry that he couldn't be a bit more understanding. He told her he was going back to LA in a couple of weeks and he'd go alone if she couldn't go with him: his next-to-youngest daughter would be celebrating her twenty-first and he wanted to be there for her. While she understood, she felt that as his new wife, he should put her needs first. He told her he'd be back the following week and by that time maybe Roy would have agreed to let her take the boys away, if only for a holiday. She'd told him not to hold his breath, Roy would never agree to that and she wasn't leaving the UK until she knew for certain that Harley and the babies were going to be alright. He'd gone off to the bedroom to sulk and by the time she came to bed, he was sleeping.

She knew deep down she'd made a big mistake in marrying Hank. What on earth had possessed her to say yes? Less than two weeks and she was already regretting it. But the alternative wasn't much better – spending months alone here with the boys. Maybe in time things would get easier and Roy would either back down and give her full custody, or allow her to come and go as she pleased with the little ones. A few months here and a few in LA until they started school would be ideal.

She'd never met anyone she wanted to spend the rest of her life with, except for Roy, and she couldn't have him. Being with Hank was a bit like being with a best mate and she *was* very fond of him. Her first marriage to Daniel McVey had been similar. But that's not how marriage should be, she thought. Or maybe it was and she was expecting too much. Hank was loving enough, but the passion she knew she should feel just wasn't there. She helped herself to a glass of milk and went into the lounge.

Harley's handbag lay on the floor beside the sofa. Damn, if she'd spotted it earlier, they could have taken it to the hospital. She picked up the bag; it was unzipped and the contents spilt onto the floor – mobile phone, flashing with unanswered messages, lipstick, hairbrush and a bunch of car keys with house keys attached. The three almost identical Yale keys had tiny stickers on each one; labels with names: Dad's, Mom's, Jess's. Livvy hesitated for a few seconds and removed the Dad one. She pushed the rest of the keys to the bottom of the bag, put the phone in the little inside pocket and did up the zip, her hand folding around the key she'd taken. Harley wouldn't miss it for a while; she certainly wouldn't need it to let herself in and out of Roy's place for a few weeks and somehow she'd find a way of replacing it before then. Roy and Sammy would be spending a lot of time at the hospital over the next few days, an ideal opportunity to go and look for the boys' passports.

* * *

'Roy!' Sammy shook him by the shoulder. She put two mugs of coffee on the bedside table, slid into bed beside him and rubbed her hand over his bristly chin. He stirred and smiled sleepily, reaching for her. 'Jack just called,' she told him.

He sat up. 'And?'

'Harley's had a good night, her blood pressure has come down a bit. She's booked for theatre at one. He'll call us with an update as soon as he can.'

'So they're still going ahead with the caesarean?'

'Yes.' He looked so anxious, her heart went out to him. 'Don't worry, love, they'll look after her. Everything will be fine. They told Jack that if they don't do this, the placenta will start to fail and Harley would be at risk of fitting. There's no other option and there's nothing we can do now except keep calm and wait. Jack said he'd let Livvy know. Hopefully they'll allow us to visit this evening.'

He nodded. '*I'll* give Livvy a call later too. I want to know what happened at her lawyer's meeting.'

'I doubt she'll tell you very much.' Sammy handed him his coffee and leant back against the headboard, sipping hers. She loved early mornings when the house was empty and it was just the two of them. So peaceful and a rare event. Better make the most of it while they still could. 'I think we should start looking at bigger houses this week,' she added after a few minutes. 'If Livvy decides to go back to LA with Hank, and the boys come to us until things are sorted, and Harley, Jack and the babies come to live with us permanently, we've no space to accommodate them all. And then there's Courtney too, although she could buy half the houses in Cheshire with what she inherited from her father.'

'Courtney's not really our concern: she's an adult. She can move in with Jamie's folks for now and we'll manage here just fine,' Roy said. 'It'll be a bit of a squeeze, but we've enough on our plate at the minute without the mither of moving.' He gave her the lazy smile that she loved and his dark eyes twinkled. 'Well, at least you won't be able to chuck me out of our bed when I can't sleep!'

'I didn't chuck you out, you big baby! I needed my sleep, even if *you* didn't. You finished?' She took his empty mug, put it on the bedside table with hers and pulled him down beside her.

He wrapped his arms around her and sighed into her hair. 'I'm a nervous wreck, Sam. Be glad when today's over.'

'I know,' she whispered, cuddling closer. 'Let's try and take our minds off things for a while.'

* * *

Jack slid back into the delivery suite, smoothing down his green disposable gown. He adjusted the elasticated cap that covered his unruly curls and smothered his hands in liquid from the bottle hanging by the door. Taking a deep breath, he made his way to a chair next to the top of the bed that Harley lay on.

'Not long now, Jack,' a pleasant-faced midwife said. 'You sure you'll be alright?'

He nodded and reached for Harley's hand. He felt nervous, sick and excited all at the same time. 'You okay, Harls?'

She smiled, but her brown eyes looked anxious. 'The spinal block has kicked in. I'm numb now, I can't feel my tummy or my feet.'

Jack chewed his lip, feeling beads of sweat break on his forehead. The theatre doors swung open and Mr Garner, Harley's obstetrician, dressed in blue scrubs, walked in. Trolleys, set with instrument trays, were pushed towards the bed. Jack watched as a young midwife removed the sterile lids from the trays.

Mr Garner smiled at Harley and Jack. 'How are we doing?' he asked Harley, snapping on a pair of latex gloves.

'Fine, thank you. I just want it over now,' she said. 'Remember you said I wouldn't have a big scar and I want it—'

'Below the bikini line,' Mr Garner finished for her. 'I know. And I'll do my very best. Be all done before you know it. You okay up there, Jack?'

Jack nodded as Harley's tummy was painted with a bright yellow liquid and Mr Garner and the two midwives put on face masks. The doors opened again and three people walked in, wearing the blue scrubs of theatre staff.

The pediatrician and neonatal team nodded as they assembled in the stifling room.

'What's the yellow stuff?' Jack asked.

'Iodine,' the midwife told him. 'It'll wash off in time.'

'Thank goodness for that,' Harley said, her voice wobbling. 'This is it, Jack. Not quite what I envisaged giving birth would be like, but still...'

Jack squeezed her hand, fighting the queasy feelings. It felt so hot in the theatre and the lights above the bed were bright and threw out heat too. He hoped he wouldn't faint, not like Harley's dad had done at her birth, or so she'd told him. He blinked as Mr Garner wielded a scalpel. Jack took several deep breaths and stroked Harley's forehead. He couldn't really see what was happening further down as Harley was covered with plastic drapes that obscured his view. He swallowed hard as the obstetrician delved with both hands through a hole in the middle of the drapes and lifted out a tiny dark-haired baby. The cord was cut and clamped and the baby placed in a clear plastic bag, like the sort Jack had seen his mum cook chickens in. One of the neonatal nurses gave Jack and Harley the first glimpse of their tiny round-faced son.

Tears ran down Jack's cheeks as the baby opened his mouth and took a first breath. 'Is he okay?' Jack asked as a thin wail filled the air. 'Why is he in that bag?' He looked on as the baby was rushed across to a table and quickly examined and weighed by the pediatrician.

'He's fine, just a fraction over three pounds, so he's done well,' the midwife called over her shoulder. 'The bag's to keep him warm,' she told Jack and placed the baby in a plastic crib with a clear lid.

Mr Garner lifted out the second baby, a girl, who was also dark-haired – but silent. He handed her to the second midwife, who bagged her and took her across to the table where both the midwives and the neonatal nurses crowded round.

After what felt like hours but in reality was a few seconds, a reedy cry sounded and Jack let out a long breath.

'Thank God for that,' he whispered. 'They're so tiny, I'll be terrified of touching them.'

'Hope they're okay,' Harley said, her eyes filling with tears.

'Three pounds, dead on,' the midwife called as she weighed their little daughter and placed her in a crib next to her brother. 'Not bad weights at all. They would have been big babies at full term. We'll take them down to the neonatal unit now, where they'll stay for a few weeks. They'll be given help with their breathing and feeding. Now then, names... Have you decided?'

Harley nodded. 'Yes, as soon as we knew what we were having we chose, but kept it secret. He's Benjamin Edward, after Jack's pops and great-granddad.'

'And she's Molly Jane after Harley's gran and my gran,' Jack said proudly.

'So it's Ben and Molly Mellor,' Harley said, a big smile on her face.

'How lovely,' the midwife said. 'Nice to keep it in the family. Some of the names chosen these days would make your hair curl! Right, I'll put their names on wristbands and we'll get on our way. Mr Garner will stitch Harley and we'll get her settled. You can take her down to see the babies when she's had a rest, Jack.'

'Do you want to go and phone everyone while he finishes sorting me out, Jack?' Harley suggested. 'I know you've struggled, you're white as a sheet. At least you did better than my dad! Get out of those clothes and find some fresh air as well. I'll see you back in my room in a while.'

Jack bent to kiss her and whispered, 'I love you. I'm so proud of you. God – Harley – we're parents!'

'I know!' She laughed and kissed him back. 'Now the fun begins.'

'We'll have the best time of our lives, I promise,' he said.

* * *

Roy put the phone down and waltzed Sammy around the kitchen. Jack had just called: the babies had arrived safely and Harley was doing fine.

'So come on, weights, names...' Sammy demanded, laughing at his excitement.

'Err, tiny, erm! Call Jess, she'll know. I can't remember, I didn't take it all in. Three pounds or something like that. Sam, you know I'm crap at that sort of thing,' he said as she tutted and shook her head. 'Names though – Ben and Molly, with Edward and Jane tacked on.' He pulled her close as her eyes filled with tears. Her late mother, Molly, had passed away the previous year and six months earlier, Jane had lost her father, Ben. 'I know that will mean the world to you and Jane,' he said as she nodded tearfully. 'And Ed will be chuffed to bits with his namesake.'

* * *

Livvy pulled over and grabbed her cell phone. 'Jack?' She listened as he relayed the events of the last couple of hours then breathed a sigh of relief. 'So everything's okay? Thank God for that! Congratulations, Jack, and give Harley my love. Can we visit tonight?'

Jack told her he'd call her later. He wasn't sure if Harley would be up to too many visitors today but he was sure she'd be alright by tomorrow and maybe they should all take turns as his mum and dad and Roy and Sammy and his grandparents all wanted to visit too. He and Harley would work out a rota for the first few days.

'No worries, just let me know. I've got her handbag at home – she left it behind. Her phone's in it. She'll want to text her friends, no doubt. I'll wait until I hear from you and then either bring it to the hospital or drop it off at Roy and Sammy's place. See you soon.'

Livvy ended the call and sat for a minute to savour the wonderful feeling of being a new grandma. She called her parents in Glasgow and related the news to them and then rang her best friend Sheena and told *her*, ending with a promise to call her back later with an update. She still hadn't told her parents or Sheena about her marriage. That was something she'd need to do sooner rather than later as they'd all want to come down and see the babies.

Head ringing with congratulations, she continued on her way into Wilmslow, where she planned to order flowers for Harley and get a key cut. At least then she could put Harley's key back on the key ring and not worry about rushing to get into Sammy's place to look for the boys' passports. There'd be ample opportunity to do that over the next few days when Jack sorted out his visiting rota.

6

Harley held her son's tiny hand through the opening at the side of the incubator. She watched as his chest moved rhythmically up and down with the help of a mechanical ventilator. The nasogastric tube up his nose was taped to his cheek and a little blue knitted hat helped keep in the heat. She looked across at Jack, who was sitting next to Molly's incubator, a devoted look on his face. She smiled. He was besotted with his daughter already. Also on oxygen, Molly was much livelier than Ben, wriggling constantly so that her tiny pink hat slipped over her eyes.

The twins had spent five days in neonatal care and appeared to be doing well. The staff had told Harley that tomorrow they would be taken off the ventilators and she and Jack would be shown how to give them a bottle feed. It was a daunting thought, the fact that they would need to hold them for more than the few minutes they'd been allowed so far, but as soon as they weighed around five pounds they could go home. She'd even managed to supply them with her own breast milk, painful though it was to express it with the contraption they'd given her. But at least she knew she was doing her best for her babies and that was the main thing.

'I'm starving,' Jack said, rubbing his stomach. 'It's ages since breakfast.'

Harley nodded. 'Me too. We should go back to my room. Mum and Dad will be here in a few minutes with the picnic lunch they promised.'

Jack's face lit up. 'Great. I'm sick of hospital food.'

'Not the best, is it? Come on then, chauffeur, help me to the wheelchair. We'll come down after lunch and Mum and Dad can have a peep at them through the windows.'

* * *

Sammy laid out a selection of sandwiches, quiche and cakes on the bedside table. 'Get stuck in,' she said as Jack made Harley comfortable on the bed. Roy brought in a couple of stacking chairs from the corridor and he and Sammy sat down. She poured coffee from a flask into mugs from home.

Jack stretched out on the bed beside Harley and picked up a mug. He closed his eyes and savoured the aroma. 'Wonderful! That crap from the vending machine is doing my stomach no favours.'

'Columbian, Jack. Your favourite,' Sammy said.

'You're so thoughtful. Best mother-in-law I've got,' Jack quipped.

Harley's phone rang out as they tucked in. 'Mom,' she said, checking the screen. 'Excuse me while I speak to her.'

Sammy caught Roy's raised eyebrow and frowned. She hoped Livvy wouldn't come and spoil their visiting time. She was dying to see the babies again, even if it was only through glass, and selfish though it might be, she didn't want to share their special moment with Livvy.

'See you later then,' Harley finished and ended the call. 'Just confirming her visit with Courtney tonight,' she told them.

'Okay.' Sammy nodded, relieved. 'Thought she might be queue jumping. I'm going over to see Jane and Jess tonight. Both of your dads, Ed, Jason and Nathan are planning a head-wetting at the pub.'

'Why don't you come with us, Jack?' Roy suggested. 'We can put you in a taxi back here later.'

Jack looked at Harley: 'That okay with you? Would you mind?'

'Course not. It's what men do and it'll give you a chance to catch up with your brother. You haven't seen much of Nathan lately. I can talk gory birth details with Mom. Sorry, Dad,' she added, laughing as Roy pulled a face. 'Jack, stay at your mum's tonight. I'll probably go to sleep early and you'll only stumble around and cause chaos if you've had a few too many. They might not even let you back in late. Do you good to relax for a few hours.'

'Good idea,' Roy agreed. 'You'll be legless when we've finished with you. It's a double celebration, after all. And you won't get many chances to do that once the babies are home.'

'Didn't stop you and Eddie,' Sammy reminded him, eyebrows raised.

Roy grinned and reached for a sandwich. 'Don't exaggerate. We were away with the group most of the time while the kids were little. I'm going to enjoy your babies, Harley. Little Molly reminds me of you.'

Harley smiled. 'Jack thinks Ben looks like RJ. Considering they're not identical, they *do* look very much alike.'

Sammy nodded, glad deep down that the twins were dark like the Cantellos and not blonde like Livvy. She immediately felt guilty for having such thoughts. The very fact they were alive and doing well should be enough. She urged everyone to eat up and then busied herself packing away the leftovers. 'Do you have any laundry to take home, Harley? And is there anything we can bring in tomorrow?'

'Yeah, there's stuff in a bag in the locker,' Harley said. 'And, erm...' She looked at her dad and blushed slightly.

'Women's talk?' he teased. 'Come on, Jack, let's leave them to it. Stretch our legs and I'll have a fag while we're outside.'

Harley waited until her dad and Jack had left the room.

'What is it?' Sammy asked, rummaging in the locker.

Harley rubbed her chest and her eyes filled with tears. 'I'm in agony, Mum. That blinking breast pump kills. I'm leaking milk all the time in-between using it. The breast pads they gave me are far too thin. And look, my boobs are nearly down to my knees!'

Sammy gave her a gentle hug; remembering back to the births of her own babies and how upset she'd felt when her previously pert breasts resembled rugby balls for weeks. 'We'll call at Boots on the way home and get you some decent pads. It won't be for long, sweetheart, and you're doing right by your babies. It'll all be worth it in the end.'

Harley wiped her eyes on her dressing-gown sleeve. 'I'm just being a mard baby. Could you get me a couple of magazines, too? Something nice and glossy, with lots of clothes and shoes. I need to remind myself what it'll be like to wear normal things again. That's if I ever get back to my old size.'

'Course you will. You can see a difference already. A few more weeks and you'll be wearing your skinny jeans. And you're not being a mard baby, your hormones are all over the place at the moment.'

'Can't wait to hold Jack close again. First the bump got in the way and now I can't bear him to come near me because of the discomfort and pain.'

'I'm sure, but like I say, it won't be for long. No doubt your mother and Courtney will be able to cheer you up later.'

Harley shrugged. 'Doubt it. Mom's in her own little world

at the moment. Don't know what's going on in her head. Maybe
it's with being newly-wed and she's all wrapped up in Hank.
And Courtney and Jamie are off on their travels again soon.
They're going to South America next. Well, that's the plan
anyway.'

'You sound almost envious,' Sammy said, frowning.

'Oh no, I'm not envious. I wouldn't swap my babies for
anything. When they're old enough, Jack and I will show them
the world. We plan to do so much with them. First things first
though: we need to get them back to Ashlea Grange and enjoy
being a proper family.'

Sammy bit her lip. Livvy still hadn't told her girls about her
long-term plans. Nor the fact that Harley and Jack and the
babies would be coming to live at the cottage on their discharge
from hospital. The decorator was due to start the nursery
makeover soon. Roy still wouldn't agree to an extension. God
only knew why. It certainly wasn't the money, but he was being
so obstinate about it to the point where she might just have to
take matters into her own hands.

* * *

Roy brought a tray of drinks to the noisy crowd assembled in
The Royal Oak's lounge. He placed the tray on a table and
picked up a pint of lager. 'So, raise your glasses to Molly and
Ben, new father Jack, grandpa Jon, uncles Jason and Nathan,
great-grandpops Ed and grandpa me! Here's to a healthy and
happy life for all.' Glasses were clinked and lager knocked
back.

'Great to get the chance to all have a drink together,' Eddie
said. 'Pity Tim's away and Jules couldn't come.' He looked at
Jason.

'Somebody has to look after her ladyship,' Jason said. 'Jules
doesn't mind – he likes having Daisy all to himself occasionally.

She's going to see the babies tomorrow afternoon with me, she's very excited.'

'Mine and Jane's turn tomorrow night,' Eddie said. 'Jack's very organised with his rota system. Who's there tonight?'

'Livvy and Courtney,' Roy said.

'Courtney didn't turn up,' Jack announced. 'Livvy and Hank had an argument and he went out and didn't come back to look after the boys. So Courtney stayed home to babysit and Livvy came on her own. She looked a bit upset actually. No doubt she'll tell Harley what's wrong.'

'Things not going well with her and Hank then?' Eddie asked Roy.

Roy shrugged. No doubt the argument was about going to LA, but he couldn't discuss it with Ed in front of Jack, who was still unaware of the situation. The lad had enough to cope with at the moment. Livvy needed to put Harley in the picture soon so she could get used to the fact that she would be bringing the babies to the cottage when they left hospital. The sooner he could get Sammy into Jasmine House and hand the cottage keys to Harley and Jack, the better.

'Ready for another?' Roy got to his feet.

'My round,' Eddie said and downed the last of his pint.

Roy accompanied him to the bar and voiced his thoughts.

'Hmm, you don't think she'll do a runner with the kids, do you?' Eddie said.

'No, she can't. We've got the passports. She's just pissed off with me because I won't let her take them. It was her choice to marry the bloke; if she wants to be with him, she can bugger off – on her own. But how she can even think of leaving Harley and those babies is beyond me. That girl needs her. Livvy's changed – she's more head-in-the-clouds than ever. Thank God I'm out of it.'

'Harley's got Sammy,' Eddie said. 'She's always been more of a mother to her than Livvy will ever be.'

'She has, and Harley knows that.' He turned as someone whistled across the room and he and Eddie were joined by Phil Jackson, The Raiders' blond-haired rhythm guitarist, who slung his arms around their shoulders, his blue eyes twinkling. 'Hey, mate, didn't know if you could make it,' Roy greeted him.

'Wouldn't miss it for the world. Well done, Grandpa, and you too, Great-grandpops,' Phil said, laughing. 'So, the Mellor and Cantello clans are finally blood-related. When Kate and Zak produce, Ed and I will be related too,' he added, referring to his son who was married to Eddie's youngest daughter. 'Don't know any other group with so many interrelated family members. We should try for the *Guinness World Records*! Kate showed me photos – proper little Cantellos they are too.'

Eddie grinned. 'Couldn't really mistake them, could you?'

Roy smiled. 'They did well, Jack and Harley. Considering what they've been through. I'm proud of them both. Right, let's get the round in, try and get Jack drunk – he needs to relax on his night off.'

* * *

'You okay, Mom?' Harley asked. Her mom looked miles away, not that it was anything out of the ordinary lately. But she was more so tonight. Harley stared as Livvy looked down at her hands, clasped together round her denim-clad knees. When she looked up, there were tears in her eyes.

'I've something to tell you, sweetie.'

'What's that?' Harley prompted, frowning. Her mom looked really sheepish. Then a sudden thought struck her: 'Mom, you're not... erm, pregnant, are you?'

'If only it were that simple,' Livvy muttered and shook her head. 'Hank had a vasectomy years ago and with eight kids between us, I think we've got quite enough. I, erm, I'm going to live in LA with Hank and the boys.'

Harley stared at her in silence for a few seconds. 'LA? But why? I thought Hank was planning to live with us all at The Grange. What changed his mind? And can't you change it back again?'

'He didn't change his mind, honey – that was always the plan. I'm sorry I didn't tell you sooner. Your dad refuses to let me take the boys out of the country but I'm fighting him for custody. I told Courtney this before I came here tonight. That's why Hank and I had a fight and he stormed out. I need to make things right before he goes to LA for his daughter's birthday next week. Otherwise, I don't think he'll come back to me.'

Harley didn't know what to say. She could feel tears starting. Surely her mom wouldn't leave the boys, but if Dad said she couldn't take them there wasn't much choice. Not if she wanted to hang onto her new husband. 'Mom, I don't want you to go. You said you'd never leave me again, that you'd always be here for me. And what about my babies? Don't you want to see them grow up?'

Livvy sobbed into her hands. 'I don't want to go, honey. I'd rather Hank lived here with us, but he wants to be with his family too. I shouldn't have married him, I know that now. We've both got too much baggage. But I can't just give up, can I? If I do, it means your dad's won again. Wrecked my life even further. I can't handle him being with Sammy and he knows it. That's the truth. I think Hank also struggles with the fact that Roy lives only a few miles away – he knows I still have feelings for him.'

'I guess it would help if you didn't live so close, but LA, Mom! You can't do that. I don't want to lose my little brothers either,' Harley cried. 'And with two small babies, it's unlikely Jack and I will be able to visit very often. What does Courtney say?'

'The same as you. But like I pointed out, she and Jamie are

going to be away again for months and then there's talk of them going to Australia for a year or two after South America.'

'So I'm to be left with no family on my mother's side,' Harley said, knowing she sounded needy, but trying to sway things her way.

'There's my mum and dad in Glasgow. You can invite them to stay and I promise to come back often to see you and the twins.'

'But it won't be the same. And will Dad sell the house? Where will we live?' Harley sniffed back tears and reached for a tissue from the locker.

'You're going to live with your dad and Sammy at the cottage,' Livvy said.

Harley shook her head. 'There's not enough room. And if Dad gets the boys, where the hell will he put us all? And there'd be no chance of inviting Granny and Grandpa. They'd have to sleep in a tent! And do Mum and Dad already know you're going? Why didn't they tell me?' She could feel her voice rising and choked on a sob.

Livvy sighed and held Harley's hands. 'They felt it was up to me to tell you. Maybe it's time you and Jack had a place of your own. I'll speak with Roy and tell him your concerns.' The end-of-visiting bell rang and she got to her feet. 'I'll call in at the cottage on the way home, let him and Sammy know that I've told you my plans.'

'He won't be there and neither will Mum. Dad's wetting the twins' heads, that's why Jack's not here. And Mum's with Jane at Hanover's Lodge tonight.'

'Oh... well, I'll call them tomorrow. I'll go and make peace with Hank now. See you soon, sweetie.' She bent to kiss Harley and left the room.

Harley flopped back on her pillows and stared at the ceiling. For crying out loud, why did everything have to be so bloody complicated with her family? She and Jack needed one more year of living with parents and then they planned to move on when he finished his studies. There was no way they could impose on Dad and Sammy for that long, especially if they won custody of her little brothers. She'd no doubts her dad would buy them a place to live, but they'd still have running costs and Jack wanted them to stand on their own two feet once he was earning. In fact, he was insistent on it. Maybe his mum and dad could squeeze them in, or his grandpops and Jane. They had spare rooms at Hanover's Lodge. She wished now that Jack was coming back tonight, she needed to talk with him. Her head was thumping and she felt all churned up inside.

Livvy pulled up outside Sammy's cottage. She'd driven around the area, waiting until it got a bit darker. She peered through the windscreen: no lights on inside, just the outside light, which she figured must be on a time switch. She drove slowly away and parked her Mercedes saloon a bit further down the lane in a lay-by. What a stroke of luck that she'd mentioned calling here to Harley. Highly unlikely Roy and Sammy would be back before midnight. When Roy got stuck in for a session he'd be in the pub until last orders and would probably go back with Eddie in a taxi to Hanover's Lodge to collect Sammy. It was only ten now, that should give her a couple of hours at least.

She reached over to the back seat for her black fleecy jacket, slipped it on, tucked her curls up inside the hood and got out of the car. She slunk back down the lane, keeping close to the over-grown hedge. The gates to the drive stood open. Roy's BMW and Sammy's Porsche were parked in front of the double garage. Fortunately, the detached cottage had no immediate neighbours. The gravel drive crunched beneath her cowboy boots so she side-stepped onto the soil of the flower border and made her way to the front door. She glanced back towards the gate, making sure no one was in the vicinity, dog-walking or jogging. She looked up at the cottage, took a deep breath and dug the newly cut key out of her jeans pocket. What if the burglar alarm was on? Damn, she'd not given that a thought until now; fancy getting this close and then remembering something so important. She chewed her lip. Dare she even try the door? If the alarm went off, she'd make a run for it. People tended to ignore alarms for the first ten minutes anyway and she'd be well away by the time the neighbours down the lane arrived.

Her own alarm number was 1985, the year of Harley's birth. Would Sammy have chosen something as simple as Jason or Nick's birth years? Well, it would be easy enough to try both as they'd been born with only ten months between them. Her legs felt like jelly and the butterflies in her stomach fluttered crazily. She took another deep breath, pushed the key into the lock and opened the door. A beeping sounded immediately and although she'd only been to the cottage a few times she recalled the alarm pad was on the wall by the large mirror. She pressed in 1966 – Nick's birth year – and the beeping stopped. She closed the door behind her, leant against it and felt tears of relief run down her cheeks.

7

Sammy put down her glass and picked up a tortilla chip. She reached for the jar of salsa and dipped into it.

'Ready for a refill?' Jane indicated her empty wine glass towards Sammy's. 'You too, Jess?'

'Please, Mum.' Jess placed her glass on the coffee table. 'You okay, Sam?' she asked as her mum left the room. 'You're very quiet. Was everything alright at the hospital?'

'Sorry,' Sammy said. 'I was miles away. Harley was a bit upset – she's got sore and leaky boobs. She'll be fine in a week or two when things settle down. Those breast pumps seem to stimulate more than normal breastfeeding does. The babies are coming on a treat. Bet they'll be home in a week or two. Little Molly is a right fidget, but Ben seems really placid, a typical laid-back male!'

'Molly will be just like Harley,' Jane said, returning with an open bottle of Chardonnay. She topped up their glasses and sat down. 'With a bit of luck, Ben will be nice and quiet like Jack is. Let's hope he's got none of Nathan's traits.'

'God help them if he does,' Jess said dryly. Nathan had always been the handful between her sons; Jack had been a dream to bring up. 'When are you going to tell them they're not going home to Ashlea Grange, Sam?'

'I'm not,' Sammy replied. 'That's up to Livvy. She's the one doing the runner; she needs to prepare the ground. I've arranged for the decorator to update the nursery and Roy and I went to John Lewis and ordered carpet and curtains and all the other paraphernalia. They're delivering next week.'

'Where the heck are you going to put it all?' Jane picked up a handful of cashews. 'And more to the point, all the kids?'

'Well, that's the problem,' Sammy said. 'I don't really know. Roy's got a right stubborn head on at the moment. He won't discuss an extension even though he bloody well knows we need one.' She stopped as Jane and Jess exchanged glances. 'What? Has he said something?'

'Not to me,' Jane said and Jess shook her head.

'Well, he's doing my head in so I've made a decision while I was in the taxi coming here. I'm going to call the guy who reno-vated the cottage for me. He knows the layout of the place and where the pipework and stuff are. I'm hoping we can build out over the top of the garage – two bedrooms and another bath-room – and at the back of it, another sitting room so that Jack and Harley *and* us can have a bit of privacy. They can invite friends over then without Roy grumbling that the house is always full of youngsters.'

'Sounds like a plan.' Jane nodded. 'Think you should discuss it with Roy though before you hire the guy.'

Sammy snorted. 'No point, he'll change the subject.' She was quiet for a moment, then, 'Something's just struck me. He hasn't said anything, but I hope he doesn't think we're all moving into Ashlea bloody Grange when *she* goes! Because if he does, he can move in on his own with the kids. There's no way I'll live in the same house he's lived in with *her*.' She picked up her glass and took a sip of wine. 'And another thing, *I'm* paying for the extension. It's my house, my money, *his* kids, so there's no way he should be objecting when it benefits us all. I don't care how much it costs, it's being done!'

Jane held up her hands in resignation. 'You're as stubborn as he is! Erm, maybe we could have Jack, Harley and the babies here while you crack on with your plans. We've loads of space. I think we need to sit down and discuss this with *them* and Ed and Roy. But let's hang on until Livvy's had a word with them about her plans – we don't want Harley getting upset while she's a mass of hormones.'

* * *

Livvy slipped the hood of her jacket off and stood on the landing, staring at all the closed doors. She'd switched on the light, hoping that anyone walking past the house would assume Roy and Sammy were home. After all, the cars were outside. Which room would be theirs? Master bedrooms were usually at the front of the house. She opened one of the doors and flicked the light on. Guest room, too small for a master, probably the one Harley and Jack used when they stayed over, no doubt the one they'd be spending the next few months in too. Neatly furnished and tastefully decorated in Sammy's favoured minimalist style and neutral tones.

She spotted clothes on the back of a tub chair and recognised them as an old Raiders' tour T-shirt that Roy often wore and a pair of Levi's. She picked up the T-shirt, held it to her nose and caught a whiff of his evocative citrus cologne; the scent still made her stomach flip. Would she ever be over him? She put the T-shirt back exactly as she'd found it. Why would he get changed in the spare room, if indeed that's what he'd done? Surely he and Sammy weren't sleeping separately after all the effort in getting back together? She turned the duvet back on the leather sleigh bed. The sheet underneath was slightly creased, a sign that it had been slept on. The pillows too had faint indentations. She picked one up and got another whiff of citrus.

A smile played on her lips. Trouble in paradise? Now wouldn't that be something? Perhaps she and Hank weren't the only ones with problems. She left the room and closed the door behind her. The second door revealed Roy's music room, stacked to the beams with amps and guitar cases. A third door revealed a family bathroom and a fourth her sons' nursery with its colourful *Thomas the Tank Engine* themed décor.

She grasped the brass knob of the last door and turned it. The door swung open to reveal the large master bedroom, decorated and furnished in a more traditional style. The huge brass bed, neatly made up, was piled high with silk cushions in varying shades of cream and purple. She slipped inside. There was stuff of Roy's in here too; leather jacket on the back of a chair, jeans folded on the seat and a guitar lay on top of an antique captain's chest under the window. She chewed her lip. Maybe they'd had a fight one night and Sammy had ordered him out of the bedroom. Whatever, she'd love to know the reason why he'd slept in the spare room.

Now where would he keep his old-fashioned black briefcase? She'd bet her life on it that the boys' passports were in there. He'd always kept bank statements, birth certificates and passports in it when he'd lived with her. When she'd teased him about its ancient state, and said that she'd buy him a new one, he'd told her the case had belonged to his Italian grandfather. A quick glance around and she couldn't see it lying about. A run of wardrobes filled the back wall. She slid open the first door. Sammy's clothes; hanging neatly from two rails, one above the other. Colour-coordinated tops, sweaters and several pairs of immaculately pressed designer jeans. She shook her head. Typical Sammy. Who the hell irons jeans? The next door revealed dresses, jackets and coats. Roy's wardrobes held haphazardly-hung shirts and jeans, some even heaped in a pile at the bottom. She smiled. He'd always been an untidy sod. Looked like Sammy had given up trying to house-train him. A row of shelves next to his clothes was crammed with papers and files. She looked up and there on the top shelf sat the briefcase. Fantastic! But how the heck was she going to reach up there?

The bedroom chair was the only option. She removed Roy's clothes, threw them on the bed and struggled to carry the chair across the room rather than leave drag marks in the deep-pile carpet. Clambering onto it, she stretched up, wobbling slightly on the soft upholstered seat. She grabbed a corner of the brief-case and yanked. It fell to the floor as she lost her grasp. She jumped down and nearly cried with relief as the catches sprang open when she tried them. The key had probably been lost years ago. She rooted inside, scrabbling through batches of documents, filed in pleated compartments, and pulled out a brown envelope with 'Danny and RJ's passports' written on the front in Roy's scrawling handwriting. She checked inside the envelope then put it on the floor and re-fastened the case. She balanced on the chair again and struggled to push the bulky case back onto the shelf, wishing, not for the first time, that she was at least three inches taller. One final push and it slid into place, just as she overbalanced and fell backwards, cracking her head on the corner of the captain's chest.

She lay stunned on the floor for what felt like ages before struggling to sit up. She felt sick and put her hand to the back of her head. Her hair felt sticky and she saw blood on her hand when she pulled it away. 'Oh no!' she muttered, staring at the patch of blood on the light-beige carpet. She got slowly to her feet and made her way on shaky legs out to the bathroom. A packet of baby wipes sat on the windowsill. She reached for a handful and dabbed at her head. She was about to flush the wipes down the loo when she remembered the cottage had a septic tank. Better take them home in her handbag rather than create problems. But what to do about the carpet? She couldn't

leave wet cloths lying around and Roy and Sammy were bound
to walk on the damp patch later. She grabbed a roll of toilet
paper and the pack of wipes and made her way back to the
bedroom. Down on her knees she felt groggy and hoped she
wouldn't pass out as she blotted and rubbed at the blood. She
did her best; it would have to do. She needed to get out of there
before she had any further mishaps. Where the devil did
Sammy keep her hairdryer? It would take most of the damp out.
She pulled open the drawers of a large chest and found it. Sock-
ets? She found one, unplugged the bedside lamp and set to. It
seemed to take forever, but eventually looked okay and maybe
in the subdued light from the bedside lamps would be unno-
ticeable.

She checked her watch: just after eleven. Better make a
move in case they decided to come back early. Remembering to
turn off all the lights and put the wipes and bloodstained loo
paper into her bag, Livvy made her way downstairs, sorted the
burglar alarm and made her way back up the lane to her car.
She sank into the soft leather seat and closed her eyes. Her head
was pounding and her hair felt very wet and sticky. Bloody hell,
what if she needed stitches? And she couldn't remember now if
she'd checked to see if there was any blood on the corner of the
captain's chest. There was no way she could face going back
inside the cottage. What if she passed out in there? The chest
was dark wood and any blood, once dried, would blend in
anyway, she hoped. She started the engine and drove slowly
home.

* * *

The boys and Hank were asleep and Courtney was nowhere to
be seen when Livvy arrived back at Ashlea Grange. In the
kitchen a hastily scribbled note, propped by the coffeepot, told
her that Courtney had gone to stay at Jamie's parents' place for

the night. Hank said it was alright to go and the boys would be fine with him. *Hope that's okay with you, Mom,* the note finished. All the same if it wasn't, she thought.

She flushed the bloodied wipes and paper down the cloakroom loo and made her way upstairs. In the main bathroom she lifted her hair and struggled to take a look at the back of her head in the mirrored walls, twisting her neck from side to side with the effort. The gash was small but still bleeding. Her hair was a sticky, matted mess. She'd have to shower the blood out then pretend to Hank she'd slipped in the bathroom here and banged her head on the marble corner of the wash-basin stand. As she was about to let her hair drop down again, she gasped and touched her right ear. Shit, her gold and diamond stud, last year's Christmas gift from Harley and Jack, was missing from her lobe! She hurried back downstairs and out to her car to search, but it wasn't there, nor was it caught in the hood of her fleecy jacket.

8

Sammy smiled as she ended the call. She dropped the phone back onto the charger, turned up the radio and poured a coffee. Trevor Curtis was coming over after four. Her builder seemed as keen as her to extend the cottage. She had plenty of land at the back for a second sitting room, so there was no reason at all to be living in cramped conditions. He'd built the garage block on suitable foundations to hold anything above it. So apart from planning permission, that he'd assured her wouldn't be a problem, it was a no-brainer, as her son Jason was so fond of saying.

She felt a smug satisfaction that she'd taken matters into her own hands. The decorator was already at work in the nursery. RJ and Danny's beds had been dismantled and stored in the garage for the time being to make way for the new baby furniture. If the boys came to stay for the odd night, they could sleep on camp beds in her and Roy's room. They'd enjoy the little adventure. In fact, they had a tent, so Roy could even sleep in the garden with them if the weather stayed fine. He'd love that, *not*, she thought and grinned to herself. But it's what dads do, so he'd have to play along. It wasn't RJ and Danny's fault that he was old enough to be their grandpa.

She was dying to tell him her plans, but knew he'd pull a face, so best to wait until things were in place and then drop it gently on his toes. She checked her watch and frowned. He'd gone out ages ago to see the boys and she'd expected him back by now as they'd planned to go to The Black Boy in Prestbury for lunch. They'd have finished serving if he didn't get a move on. She tutted and dialled his number. Answerphone! Bloody hell, Roy; he knew she liked to be able to contact him when he was at Ashlea Grange. It still made her feel uncomfortable and even with Livvy safely married to Hank, that feeling would probably never go away. Husband or no husband, she didn't trust the woman one little bit. She looked up as the kitchen door opened and Mrs Melcher, the cleaning lady, strolled in: 'Coffee, Mrs M?'

'Oh please, Sammy love. I'm gasping.' Mrs Melcher pulled out a chair and dropped her well-upholstered backside onto it. She wiped her hand across her sweaty face. 'It's warm under that thatch today. I've only the windows to do in yours and the guest room and then I'm finished,' she said, spooning three sugars into the mug Sammy pushed across the table.

'Help yourself.' Sammy handed the biscuit barrel over. Mrs Melcher could eat for England and it showed but despite her bulk, she was the best cleaner they'd ever employed. She was also very loyal and Sammy knew she could trust her not to repeat anything she overheard or was told in confidence.

'Thanks, pet. That decorator's getting on with his work. The room will be done before you know it. Bet you can't wait to get the babies home. You'll have your hands full, what with the little lads and all.'

Sammy sighed. 'Tell me about it. But the boys will only be here for the odd night over the next few weeks while we get the babies settled in.'

'It'll be a bit of a tight squeeze.'

'Hmm, not if I get *my* way,' Sammy said. 'But my lips are sealed for now.'

Mrs Melcher smiled and tucked into a handful of Roy's favourite chocolate digestive biscuits. She finished her coffee and got to her feet. 'Oh, before I forget,' she said, rooting in the pocket of her flowery overall, 'this nearly went up the 'oover. It was half-hidden in the pile of your bedroom carpet, just spotted it in time.' She handed a gold and diamond stud over to Sammy and left the room.

Sammy stared at the stud, her stomach turning over. It certainly wasn't hers, but was familiar, nevertheless. It was one of a pair that Harley and Jack had given Livvy last Christmas. They'd been specially made by Courtney's boyfriend's jeweller father. They were unique in that the diamond was set into the centre of a gold square rather than a circle. What the hell was it doing in her bedroom? Surely Roy hadn't? No, he wouldn't, would he? She took a deep breath, as the room started to spin and the voice of Radio Two DJ Ken Bruce echoed in her ears. She got to her feet, ran to the under-stairs' cloakroom, closed the door and threw up her recently consumed biscuits and coffee into the washbasin. Then she sat down on the toilet and clasped her shaking hands together. 'Get a grip,' she muttered. 'There's got to be a reason other than that – he just wouldn't.' But how the hell had one of Livvy's studs ended up on her bedroom carpet? She'd never been upstairs while Sammy had been home and Harley wouldn't invite her up there. She knew how much she hated Livvy even setting foot in the cottage.

She got to her feet, rinsed the washbasin, washed her face and went back into the kitchen. She hoped Mrs Melcher and the decorator hadn't heard her being sick. How embarrassing. She dialled Roy's number again. It was still on answerphone, so she called Livvy's landline. Livvy answered. Sammy took a deep breath. 'It's Sammy. Is Roy still with you?'

'Oh, hi, Sammy. No, he left over an hour ago.'

'Okay, thanks.' Sammy hung up quickly before Livvy questioned her call. She sent Roy a curt text, asking him to get in touch.

* * *

Roy gave Jason a cheque and Jason handed over the keys to Jasmine House.

'Thanks, son,' Roy said, giving him a hug. 'You've no idea what this means to me or what it'll mean to your mum.'

'I think I can hazard a guess,' he said with a grin. 'I know Mum's been giving you a hard time lately about lack of space at the cottage and stuff. There's champagne in the fridge, candles and toiletries in the en suite. Everything's ready. When are you planning on bringing her over?'

'I was planning to wait until nearer her birthday, but I think it's going to have to be sooner. I need to get her in the right mood to suggest she hands the cottage over to Harley and Jack, at least for the foreseeable future. I know Jack has a bee in his bonnet about them standing on their own two feet. Admirable principle, but not practical with two new babies and little money coming in! I want them to have the best possible start.'

Jason nodded. 'Let me give you a quick tour before I go.' He led the way into the lounge and pointed out various features and some changes that he'd made.

Roy looked around; admiring the two huge chocolate-brown leather sofas, arranged each side of the original marble fireplace, now housing a new living-flame gas fire.

'I've put in that fire, Dad, save you messing about clearing grates when the weather's cold. Make life as easy as possible. I've left the walls picture-free so that Mum can put her own stamp on things,' Jason said. 'It's a neutral canvas so she can go mad with pictures and cushions and stuff. That sculpture by the window is from me and Jules as a house-warming gift. Do you remember the old black and white photo of you and Mum in your teens? The one that set you off blubbering on the day you were due to marry Livvy? Well, it's copied from that.'

Roy walked over to the full-size bronze sculpture of two people locked in each other's arms. He felt tears welling as he ran his hands over the waist-length hair of the female that looked for all the world like a teenage Sammy in the arms of a young man with hair styled in a neat quiff and both wearing long leather coats that were so artfully crafted, they looked almost real. There was no mistaking it for anyone other than the pair of them. How he wished they were that age again with their whole future stretching ahead. 'God, it's wonderful, son! How does Jules do it? It looks so real. Your mum's gonna be knocked out by this, probably more so than the house.'

Jason smiled. 'I'll show you your bedroom now.' He led the way upstairs and into the old master bedroom. 'I've made the bed up, just in case you decide to stay when you bring her to see it. I got you a super king, plenty of room to sprawl out. New wardrobes.' He indicated a run of fitted wardrobes down the length of a wall. 'And I've had one of the small rooms converted to a walk-in dressing room for Mum so she's got tons of space to hang her clothes.' He opened the door to the en suite. 'There you go, Dad. Top of your list! The all-important Jacuzzi.'

Roy walked into the bathroom and smiled. Jason had filled the shelves above the bath with Sammy's favourite Heavenly Gingerlily Molton Brown candles in glass holders and a wicker basket filled with matching toiletries. Even *he* loved the seductive, musky aroma and he could picture the two of them, champagne to hand, lying end to end in the scented bubbles, legs entwined, just like the old days – the before-Livvy-days – when life had been pretty blissful. He was desperate to recapture those times and he'd do his level best to make sure they did, or as near to it anyway.

Livvy had been adamant earlier that she was taking the

boys away as soon as she got custody of them. But he was standing firm. He'd told her she'd got no chance. She'd looked pale this morning and had a bandage around her head. Hank told him he wanted her to see a doctor but she snapped at him to stop fussing. Apparently she'd slipped in the bathroom last night and cut her head on the corner of the washstand. Roy had made a joke about taking more water with it next time, but it hadn't gone down very well and he'd been glad to take his leave and escape to meet Jason.

He checked his watch and realised he was running a bit later than he'd told Sammy. He pulled his phone from his jacket pocket. Fuck! It was switched off. Sammy would go mad. He'd had it on charge overnight and must have forgotten to turn it on when he left the cottage. No wonder it had been quiet all morning. When he switched it on, it beeped with messages and missed calls. All from home and Sammy's mobile. She'd be freaking out. She hated him going to Ashlea Grange, but he'd needed to see the boys and find out exactly what Livvy's lawyer had said. Not that she'd been particularly forthcoming. He pressed Sammy's mobile number. She answered immediately. He held the phone away from his ear while she ranted.

'Have you quite finished?' he interrupted. She fell silent. Was she crying? He thought he heard a sob. 'Sam, apart from being mad at me, are you okay?'

'No,' she snapped. 'Hurry up home. What's taken you so long? Are the boys alright?'

'Had something important to do,' he replied. 'And, yes, the boys are fine. They were getting ready to go to nursery so I didn't get to spend much time with them. But we're having them at the weekend, if that's alright with you?'

'Did you take them to nursery?'

'No, Hank did and, yes, before you ask, I stayed and talked to Livvy.'

'You were alone with her?'

'Well, yes. But Courtney may have been upstairs – I don't know, I didn't ask. I sat in the kitchen, had a coffee and asked Livvy a few questions. We talked about the custody case and – well – we argued mainly. Stop making a big deal, Sam.'

'I'm not. You know I hate you being alone with her, Roy.'

He could definitely hear her sobbing now and shook his head. What the hell was wrong? She was fine when he'd left her.

'I know you don't like it. I wasn't expecting that to happen, but it was unavoidable. I didn't stay long.'

'Long enough to have coffee.'

'I didn't even finish the bloody thing.'

'Well, you've been gone ages. I expected you back over an hour ago. You're always disappearing lately and you don't say where you're going. What am I supposed to think, given your track record where Livvy's concerned?'

'Fuck, Sam, what are you trying to say? No... don't even answer that. I'm coming home right now and I'm taking you out for lunch like we planned.' He ended the call and stared at Jason. 'God knows what I've done wrong now – your mother's got a right narky head on today.'

Jason patted his shoulder. 'Give her the keys, Dad. Put a smile on her face. Don't make her wait. She's got a lot on her plate, wondering where she's going to put all the kids. It's too much at her age.'

'I'll see.' Roy nodded. He said goodbye and drove home as fast as he could.

* * *

Sammy pushed her food around her plate. She couldn't really do justice to the lemon sole and seasonal veg. The Black Boy was crowded with well-heeled retirees as it always was at lunchtime. It wasn't private enough to talk. Roy had rushed her out as soon as he got home. The diamond stud was safely stashed in her handbag. Evidence for when she needed it. If he'd resumed his affair with Livvy, she'd kill him. The more she thought about it, the more convinced she was that there couldn't be another explanation for the stud being found in their bedroom. He was edgy, not meeting her eyes, as though hiding something – again. How could he? And yet… he'd been the most loving man on earth since their reconciliation, just like their early years together. Always telling her he loved her. He swore he'd never hurt her again and she really believed he meant it. But he loved his sons too and if the only way to hang onto them was to be with Livvy, then who knew? But what about Hank? Surely Livvy was happy with him? She was aware of Roy speaking to her and looked up. He'd hardly touched his meal either.

'Let's go.' He signalled to the waiter for the bill.

Outside, he took her hand. 'Fancy a little stroll around the village?'

She shook her head.

'Okay, I'll take you home then.' They made their way to the car. 'It's our turn for visiting tonight, isn't it?' he said and helped her into the passenger seat.

She nodded.

'Shall we get something to take in?' He climbed in and started the engine. 'We could pop over to John Lewis at Cheadle.'

She shrugged. 'Whatever.'

He turned to face her. 'Right, enough! Let's have it. What have I done wrong?'

She raised an eyebrow. 'Nothing, well, apart from being alone with *her*.'

'I told you that was unavoidable.'

'You should have left right away.'

'I needed to talk to her, you know that.'

'And I needed you at home – with me.' If only he'd been there when Mrs Melcher produced the diamond stud. How would he have wriggled out of that one?

'Right, well we're going home now and *you're* going to tell me why you're so narked with me.'

They drove back to the cottage in silence. Sammy could feel tears welling and could hardly breathe. She loved him so much. It would kill her to lose him to Livvy again. But she knew that to lose his boys would destroy him. Damn Livvy. She'd always have a hold over him and the bitch knew it.

* * *

Roy silently handed Sammy a mug of chamomile tea and poured himself a black coffee. They sat at the kitchen table, still silent. The decorator popped his head around the door and announced he'd be back first thing tomorrow to finish off. Roy got up to let him out.

Back in the kitchen, Roy opened the French door and stood on the patio with a cigarette. He turned back to look at Sammy, who had her mug clasped in her hands as though seeking warmth. She looked pale and he could see her shoulders shaking. What the hell was wrong with her? He stubbed his cigarette out, went to stand behind her and put both hands on her shoulders. He kissed the top of her head. As he did so, he spotted a pad on the table with 'Builder' and a phone number. 'What's that all about?' He picked it up and waved it in front of her.

She turned, her cheeks flushing slightly. 'He's coming later to give me a quote for an extension,' she replied. 'But I don't suppose there's any point now, is there?'

Roy knelt down beside her and took her hands. 'No point now? What do you mean by that?'

'Well... it's obvious.'

'Not to me. Stop talking in bloody riddles and get to the point.'

'You're going back to Livvy because you don't want to lose the boys,' she sobbed.

'What?' He almost fell backwards with shock. 'How the hell have you come to that conclusion?'

She shook her head. 'You won't agree to having a much-needed extension here. You keep going missing and I can't get hold of you and today you've been to discuss stuff with her. Hank will be going back to LA and that's it, you'll move back in with her because you don't want to lose RJ and Danny. I don't know why I didn't see it coming. Pointless me getting the house made bigger when there's only going to be me living here.'

Roy puffed out his cheeks. He got to his feet and pulled her up and into his arms. 'You're so wrong, you're miles out with your mad assumptions. Come on, get your jacket and bag, we're going out.'

'But the builder, he'll be here soon...'

'Call him and cancel the appointment.'

'But...'

'Never mind but, just do it.' He hurried out of the room and ran upstairs while she made the call. He grabbed a silk scarf from the rack in her wardrobe and pushed it into his pocket.

* * *

'Where are we going?' she asked as he sped down the lane towards Ashlea Village.

'Wait and see.'

A mile further down the road, he stopped in a lay-by, reached in his pocket and pulled out the silk scarf. Her eyes widened as he moved towards her, the scarf held between both hands.

'What are you doing?' She backed away from him.

He realised he'd scared her half to death by the terrified look in her eyes. 'Shit, Sam, I'm not going to hurt you, love! I've got a surprise. When you see it, you'll know what I've been up to for the last few weeks. Please, let me put this over your eyes until we get there.'

'A surprise?' Her voice wavered.

He nodded. 'I love you more than life itself. I don't know what's happened today to make you think it, but believe me, there's no way on earth I'm ever going back to Livvy. Please, just let me put this scarf on you as a blindfold. It'll only be for a few minutes, I promise.'

She let out a slow breath and smiled. He kissed her and tied the scarf around her eyes, smiling as she relaxed back into the seat.

Within minutes he pressed the key fob to open the electric gates, drove up the long drive and pulled up in front of their old home. 'Wait there for a second and no peeping,' he instructed as he clambered out. He hoped the crunching gravel hadn't given it away, but Ed and Jane had gravel and she might have thought they were on the way to their place. He dashed around to the passenger side and helped her to her feet: 'Are you ready?'

'Yes,' she whispered as he pressed a bunch of keys into her hand. He removed the blindfold and with a dramatic ta-da, waved his hands in the air. The look on her face was one he'd never forget for as long as he lived.

'Jasmine House,' she breathed. 'Ours? Honestly?'

He nodded, feeling tears running down his cheeks.

'Oh, Roy!' She burst into loud sobs and flung herself into his arms.

9

Sammy took several deep breaths and with Roy's arms still around her, steadied herself against the car bonnet. Her legs felt like jelly, her head pounded and her heart hammered against her ribs. She couldn't believe what he'd done. She tried to speak, but nothing came out. Roy was still crying and she ran her fingers over his cheeks to wipe the tears away. He took her hand and led her inside and through to the kitchen. She looked around, her mouth gaping. 'Oh my God! It's fabulous.' She ran her hands over the black granite worktops. The striking white kitchen was a dream. Similar to her old one in style, but with the latest of everything, including a silver, state-of-the-art American fridge that dominated one wall.

'Sit down. I'll make us some tea while you get your breath back,' Roy said, reaching for the kettle.

'Tea?' She shook her head. 'This surprise warrants more than tea, Roy.'

'Okay.' He grinned, opened the fridge and pulled out a bottle of Moët. 'Will this do?' He reached for two champagne flutes from a lit display shelf.

'Perfect,' she said, 'but let me take a look around first. I can't wait to see what you've done with our lovely home.'

He put the bottle and glasses on the worktop. 'Come and see the lounge but close your eyes and don't open them until I tell you.' He led her into the middle of the room. 'Okay, you can open them now.'

'Oh, wow!' She gazed around the spacious room with its high ceiling and ornate cornice, so familiar and yet totally new, but very her. 'I guess Jason has had a hand in this?' Chocolate, beige and ivory – he'd got it spot on. 'It's fabulous, and so me.' Her eyes moved to the bronze sculpture, and, hand to her mouth, she walked slowly towards it. She turned as Roy came up behind her and slipped his arms around her waist. He nuzzled her neck, an indulgent smile on his face.

'It's us!' she exclaimed, running her hands over the sculpture.

'It is,' he murmured. 'Wonderful, don't you think?'

'Beyond wonderful! Jules is fantastic.'

'So is our son. I left him to it and kept out of the way, except for dipping my hand in my pocket. You know I'm crap at this sort of thing.'

'I feel lost for words, Roy. I mean, just look at us then. So happy, *really* happy – I wish we could recapture our youth.'

He squeezed her tight. 'I can't give you back your youth, but we're gonna do our best to recapture the happiness we felt then – and keep hold of it this time.'

'We will,' she said, overwhelmed with love and need for him. She kissed him and whispered, 'Take me to our bedroom.'

He led her upstairs and threw open the door to the master suite.

'Oh my God!' she said again, taking in the sumptuous room, with its neutral décor and ivory silk drapes at the large bay window. She ran her hand over the chocolate-brown velvet bed throw and admired the mountain of co-ordinated cushions piled high against the brown leather headboard. 'This is amazing, just amazing!' Roy leant back against the wardrobes while she wandered around, checking each detail. She opened the door to the en suite and yelled, 'Roy, come here. A new Jacuzzi! It's much bigger than the old one. Oh, I've so missed this little luxury.'

He came into the room as she picked up a candle and held it to her nose. 'How on earth did Jason get it so right? Molton Brown candles. Perfect! Oh, and toiletries too. Wow!' She grinned at him, looped her fingers through his belt and pulled him towards the bed. 'We'll try them later, first things first.'

* * *

Sammy stirred in Roy's arms. He kissed the tip of her nose and stroked her hair off her face. 'Have I been dreaming?' she whispered. 'Are we really home?'

'We are.'

'I can't believe it. Or that you managed to keep it all secret from me. And Jason, too, he never let on. Didn't give me a clue. Not even when I was banging on about no space and needing an extension. You're such a devious pair.' She tickled him in the ribs.

He squirmed away, laughing. 'He was sworn to secrecy, like everyone else. You've screwed up my birthday surprise though. I'll have to think of something else now.'

'There's no need, this is perfect. I'm so sorry for giving you a hard time about the cottage.'

'No worries. Let's go downstairs and have a coffee. I want to show you around the rest of the place.'

'Okay.' Sammy slid out of bed and went into the bathroom. The Jacuzzi was still full and damp towels lay on the floor. She blew out the candles, emptied the bath and drew a heart on the steamy mirror, then as an afterthought wrote their initials in the heart. She smiled to herself – it was something she used to do when they were young.

'You big softie,' Roy said, standing behind her.

Jason had hung two white towelling robes on the back of the door and she lifted them down, handed one to him and slipped her arms into the other.

* * *

In the kitchen they sat at the breakfast table in front of the patio doors, drinking coffee. How many times had they done this in the past? Thousands, she thought and sighed blissfully, the gold stud in her handbag forgotten for the moment. She looked around, feeling utter contentment.

'About the cottage...' he began.

She nodded. 'I've just been thinking. I should let Harley and Jack live there. It will be a perfect first home for them and the twins, seems pointless selling it when they need a place of their own.'

'I was going to suggest the same,' he said.

'Great minds, eh? It makes perfect sense. The cottage stays in the family and we all get some space. Tons of it.' She waved her arm about. 'Even with the boys here we'll rattle around, just like we used to when Jason and Nick were small. God, I can't wait to move in! I'll bring some of my artwork and prints and leave the rest at the cottage. Harley can do what she wants with them. Tomorrow we'll go and buy all the stuff we need to finish things off here. I feel like a little girl with a new doll's house for Christmas. I love you so much for doing this. I can't tell you what it means to me – I always regretted selling this place.'

'I know you did. And I regret that you felt you had to.' He got up and walked across to the worktop, picked up an envelope and handed it to her. 'The deeds; in your name, exactly as before.'

'Roy, you shouldn't have done that,' she said, biting her lip. 'It's ours.'

He smiled. 'It's yours. You can chuck me out whenever the fancy takes you.'

'As if.' She took his hand and they wandered around, admiring the décor and furnishings in each room. In the play-room that was decked out with easels, pots of paint, small chairs, and a table, stacked high with puzzles, Roy got down on his knees and played with the Scalextric laid out on the polished wooden floor.

'Wow! Can't wait for Ed to come round and play with this, we'll have some fun.'

Sammy laughed. 'You boys, do you ever grow up?'

Roy glanced at his bare wrist: 'My watch is upstairs. No idea what time it is but I guess we'd better get dressed and make our way to the hospital.'

'Yes.' Sammy nodded. 'Can't wait to tell Harley and Jack the good news, they'll be over the moon.'

Livvy stared at Hank's back as he said goodbye and put down the phone. He turned towards her with an ear-splitting grin. 'Who was that?' she asked. He'd been talking animatedly as she'd walked into the kitchen after dropping RJ and Danny off at playgroup. She hoped he hadn't organised anything that involved going out. Her head was still aching from the bump the other night and she was looking forward to a bit of peace until the boys came home. Also, she'd just picked up a garbled message from Harley about Sammy giving her and Jack the cottage. The message had cut off before the end. She wanted to call her back and ask what it was all about. Why would Sammy do that? Where were she and Roy going? Curiosity was burning a hole in her brain.

'Our agent,' Hank said, barely able to conceal his excitement. 'He stayed up late to catch us this morning.' He paused as though for effect, then: 'Honey, you're not gonna believe this. You and me, we've only been asked to present this year's CMA Awards! What do you think to that?' He grabbed her around the waist and kissed her, hugging her tight.

She leant back in his arms and shook her head. 'I doubt we'll be able to accept.'

'What?' He loosened his grip on her. 'But we've talked about this so many times. Presenting the Country Music Awards is something we've always wanted to do.'

She shrugged and pulled away. 'I know. But this year I have to stay in the UK. There's no way I can take the boys to Nashville and I'm not leaving them with Roy and Sammy unless I absolutely have to. We haven't even got a date for the custody hearing yet. I don't want to plan anything until I know when that is. What sort of mother will I look like if I say I can't attend because I'm presenting a show?'

He frowned. 'They know what you do for a living. It shouldn't be a problem. It's not until November and it's in New York this year, not Nashville. The hearing will be over and done by then, surely?'

Livvy felt her stomach lurch and sat down heavily at the breakfast table. She hadn't set foot in New York for ages. She refused to do concerts there when the band toured, preferring theatres in Philadelphia and Boston. Her late husband had perished in the 2001 terrorist attacks on the World Trade Center and even though she and Daniel were estranged at the time, she swore she'd never visit the city again.

'I can't do it, Hank. Custody hearing aside, you know how I feel about New York.'

Hank's face tightened. He circled the table and stood in front of her. 'Isn't it time you put the past behind you?' he said, his normally soft voice rising a couple of octaves. 'Hell, Livvy, you and Daniel weren't even together at the time of 9/11! You were living with Roy and Dan was holed up with his damn PA.'

'He's still Courtney's father,' Livvy shouted back. '*And* Danny's.'

'Yeah, by pure fluke. You thought you were carrying Roy's kid. You didn't give a fuck about Daniel when you jumped into bed with lover-boy again!'

Livvy stared open-mouthed. Hank rarely raised his voice. When they had words, he turned his back and walked away rather than get into a heated argument. But he looked so angry and she realised she was pushing him too far, again, like she'd done the other night when he walked out before her visit to Harley. He'd talked many times about them presenting the CMA Awards one day and she'd always been as up for it as he was. She swallowed hard. All she'd done was push him away since their return to the UK. He was caring and patient with her – well, most of the time anyway. She knew she'd better buck her ideas up or she'd be losing him and she couldn't bear to be alone again.

She took his hand. 'I'm trying, you know. I've been through a lot in the last few years – Daniel's death, let down by Roy on my wedding day, two babies close together and dealing with Harley's illness. It all gets too much at times. I'm coping the best I can, but it's not been easy since RJ's birth.' She could feel tears sliding down her cheeks. Much as she loved her youngest son, RJ had been conceived as a saviour-sibling for Harley and was not a child she'd have had by choice. Full of mischief, he was hard work and she knew the easiest thing would be to agree that Roy and Sammy have full custody of him and she take Daniel. But he was her baby and she couldn't repeat history and just abandon him. What would people think?

Hank pulled off a sheet of kitchen roll and dabbed at her eyes. He put his arms around her and held her close. 'Let me in, Livvy,' he whispered into her hair. 'I love you and want to take care of you, but you have to let me get closer. Every time I feel I've made a breakthrough, you shut me out again. This isn't the sort of relationship I'm used to – I don't think I can handle any more unless you meet me halfway.'

'It would be so much easier if you'd stay in the UK with us,' she said, wishing she could summon up even half the feelings she still held for Roy. Hank deserved far more than she could give him.

He shook his head. 'It's not an option for me. I told you that before you agreed to marry me. Living here isn't practical for Juice and when we're not touring, I'm in session with other bands. I can't stand not working. It's driving me crazy, sitting around this place all day. Once you get custody, it'll be fine and we can start to settle as a family in LA.'

'*If* I get custody.'

He snorted. 'No court on earth will give Cantello those kids! He's too old and so is Sammy. I know I'm older than him, but you're still young *and* you're their mother.'

Livvy sighed. 'Let's hope you're right. I'll need his permission to take them out of the country though.' She wished she could tell Hank she'd got the boys' passports and once she knew that Harley and the babies were home and settled, she could take RJ and Danny wherever the fancy took her. But she was sure he wouldn't approve of her snooping around Roy and Sammy's place, so she'd keep quiet for the time being. She still felt concerned about her missing gold stud, but if she'd lost it at the cottage then she was sure it would have been found by now and something said. Chances are it fell out on the lane as she'd hurried back to the car.

She squeezed Hank's hand. 'I need to speak to Harley. I'll ring her from our room and then have a lie-down for an hour. Why don't you join me?' she added and smiled as his face lit up. 'We've got the place to ourselves. Give me ten minutes to make my call.' She left the room, thinking it wouldn't hurt her to show him some affection and she needed to feel loved herself.

* * *

Livvy smiled. Harley's excitement was evident as she told of Sammy's kind offer.

'Our own place, Mom, I can't believe it! It's so good of Sammy. She and Dad said they'll pay all our bills and everything until Jack finishes uni and gets a job. The nursery will be ready and waiting and Sammy said we could decorate the rest of the place to our own taste. I can't wait to take my babies home. By the way, I'm going home myself tomorrow, but I'll have to come back here each day to express milk and to help feed them. Jack's back at uni next week and then hopefully he'll be on holidays by the time we get home for good.' She drew breath and was quiet for a moment.

'That's wonderful news, sweetie. It's very good of Sammy to make such a gesture, but where are she and Roy going to live?'

'Oh, Mom, you're not going to believe what Dad's done! He's only gone and bought back Jasmine House for Mum's sixtieth birthday. It's been a big secret. She's absolutely made up. Jason's been working on it for weeks to get it back to how it used to be, but with all new fittings. They're moving in this weekend.' Harley fell silent, then, 'Mom, you still there?'

'Err, yes, of course I am. Well, I hope they'll be very happy. I have to go now, sweetie, Hank's calling me. I'll ring you tomorrow when you get home.' Livvy ended the call and lay back on the pillows. This was something she'd not been expecting. She sighed as Hank strolled into the bedroom and lay down beside her.

'Problem?'

'Not really. Roy's bought back Jasmine House for him and Sammy and she's given Harley and Jack the cottage.'

'That's generous of her.'

'Yeah, it is. But don't you see? Roy now has all the space in the world for the boys. I was kind of hoping to use their lack of spare rooms to help my case. You know, the overcrowding they'd have at the cottage with the kids, Harley, Jack and the twins.'

Hank shrugged. 'That wouldn't have made any difference. They'd have built an extension eventually or moved in here when we've gone. Look, why don't you ask Roy to let you bring the boys to my place for a few days for my girl's party? It's not like you won't be bringing them back to the UK. I'm really going to miss you for the next two weeks and I don't see why he gets to hold all the strings or why we should have to be apart. If he and Sammy are busy getting ready for the big move, they won't want the little ones under their feet. Just ask nicely without getting into a fight with him.'

Livvy nodded slowly. There really was no reason why she couldn't do it. No need for anyone to know. She could tell Roy she was taking the boys to see her parents and Sheena. In fact, she'd do that anyway and then fly out to the States from Glasgow. 'Maybe,' she said. 'But don't you say anything to him. I'll do the asking. I need to get their passports and I don't want him turning even more moody with me than he already is. You go as planned and I'll try and join you for a few days before the weekend.'

'Sounds good to me.' He pulled her close and kissed her.

10

Roy frowned as Livvy prattled on without stopping for breath. When she finally paused, he jumped in: 'So how long are you planning on being away?' She'd just asked his permission to take the boys on a trip to Glasgow to see her parents. 'And I was under the impression from Harley that your folks are coming down here in a week or two to see the twins.'

'Well yes, when the babies come home they will do. But Dad's back's not been too good lately and he's not up to travelling in a car or sitting on the train for hours. I thought it would be a nice change for the boys. And also I'm on my own now Hank's gone away – I fancy a few days' break myself.'

Roy took a moment to consider. It was late Monday afternoon. He'd just brought the boys home after a mad weekend with them at Jasmine House. He and Sammy had been unable to do anything while they'd entertained the pair, who'd been delighted with their new playroom. Not a single box had been unpacked and he needed time to get to grips with his new recording studio. Eddie was coming over in a couple of hours to do a bit of work with him. What harm would a visit to their

grandparents do? She'd have taken them under normal circumstances and he wouldn't have objected.

He checked his watch: 'Look, I need to get home. When are
you thinking of going?'

'Tomorrow morning. I'll have them back by next Tuesday.'

'That's a whole week. We're having a bit of a house-
warming and welcome-home-to-Harley party on Saturday –
I'd like them back for that.' He looked her directly in the eye.
She looked away and Roy saw a faint blush creep up her neck.
He frowned, wondering what that was all about. She was
made-up to the eyeballs, hair piled up with curly bits
dangling, low-cut top and short denim skirt. *So* short that
when she bent over to help RJ remove his wellies, he'd caught
a flash of her arse and a black lace thong. He shouldn't have
looked, he certainly hadn't meant to. Why did she always
dress sexy when she knew he was coming over? When would
it dawn on her that he wasn't falling for it any more? Those
killer heels were hardly the shoes to wear for running after
little kids and it wasn't as though Hank was around to appreciate her efforts. Sammy had been wearing muddy jeans, T-
shirt and trainers when he'd left her, same as he was, after a
run around the park and a duck-feeding session at the lake.
She'd promised to have the bath and herself ready for him
when he got back. He sighed inwardly feeling a rush of heat to
his groin and hoped it wasn't obvious or Livvy would be
thinking it was because of her. He realised she was speaking
again.

'Err... it's my brother Pete's birthday on Saturday. I've never
spent a birthday with him and would like to this year. Anyway,
a house-warming is hardly the sort of place for two little ones.'

'Well, it won't be a rave at our age,' he said. 'Just the band,
their wives and a few close friends. The boys love a barbecue
and Harley's hardly seen them for weeks.' The folded arms and
mutinous expression told him she wasn't buying it. He shook his

head. 'Oh, suit yourself, but make sure you bring them straight to us on Tuesday.'

'I will.' She stared at him, a look of defiance in her eyes.

He knew what was coming next: she'd have a pop at Sammy and try and start an argument. Well, he was having none of it in front of the kids.

'Isn't it time you were getting back to your wife?' she said, a sarcastic edge to her voice. 'She'll be wondering what's taking you so long! Surprised your phone's not ringing. Boys, say goodbye to Daddy, he needs to go back to Sammy now.'

Roy dropped to his knees and cuddled them close as he kissed them goodbye. He breathed in the outdoor scent of their hair and sweaty little bodies. He hated parting with them and always felt lost for a few days after.

'My come back to Sammy,' RJ said, clinging to his neck.

'Me too,' Danny cried, holding onto his arm.

'You can't,' Livvy said and pulled them away. 'Just go,' she said, pushing Roy towards the door.

He left the house, brushing an angry tear away, got into his car and looked up to see them waving from the doorstep, one each side of Livvy, clinging to her bare legs. RJ, a miniature version of his late son Nick, was crying and calling Daddy, while Danny sucked his thumb and looked sad. 'Poor little kids,' he muttered, choking on a sob. They should be with him and Sammy. They needed stability and Livvy gallivanting all over the place with them was far from right. Imagine if she got custody and he lost all parental control. She'd be leaving them with every Tom, Dick and Harry while she worked and he'd probably never see them again. He couldn't bear it. Well, it mustn't happen – that bloody solicitor had better hurry up and get his finger out.

He put his foot down and sped off towards home. He was looking forward to the jam session with Eddie later. It had been a while, what with the twins' birth and all the stuff happening with Jasmine House. Be nice to chill with a guitar in his hands, take his mind off his problems for a while. But tonight he knew he'd be listening out for a cry in the dark that wouldn't come.

* * *

Livvy finished packing suitcases and heaved them downstairs to the hall. The boys were eating tea in the kitchen and were already bathed and in pyjamas. They were tired and RJ was fractious as usual after being with Roy. It took him days to settle back down. Half an hour in front of the TV and they could go up to bed while she loaded the cases into the boot. She planned to leave at six in the morning to get a good start before the rush hour traffic. Her parents were expecting them around lunchtime and she'd arranged to go out with her friend Sheena while they looked after the boys.

She was looking forward to a bit of girlie time and a good catch-up. She still hadn't told Sheena she was married, although she'd told her mum and dad, who'd been surprised – but pleased for her. The news would be a shock for Sheena, who knew she still carried a torch for Roy.

She'd booked flights to LA from Thursday until Monday. She knew that if she could pull this trip off without Roy finding out, there was a good chance she could take them to LA and just disappear when Hank decided he was ready to return for good. They'd no doubt discuss all that and their future plans when she arrived.

All she had to do now was work out a way to stop the boys saying anything to Roy when they got home. She'd have to make out that they were play-acting at being on a plane or something if they mentioned it.

Deep down, she felt disappointed that Roy hadn't even raised an eyebrow at her after she'd made a big effort with her appearance. He'd seemed totally distant and preoccupied. His main concern, as always, had been for the boys. Well, at least she still had that over him – he would always have a link with her, whether Sammy liked it or not.

* * *

Sammy looked up as Roy walked into the kitchen. 'How did it go? Oh, Roy, come and sit down,' she said as his eyes filled. 'They'll be here again at the weekend.'

'They won't,' he said and told her about Livvy's plans. 'They'll be back next Tuesday. I told her to bring them straight here. I'm not going to her place again on my own. She was all tarted up and Hank's not there, of course – it was for my benefit, no doubt.'

Sammy shook her head. 'I told you I don't trust her. We'll do pick-ups and drop-offs together from now on.' She poured him a coffee and took his jacket out to the hall. 'Have your coffee and then come and lie on the bed with me,' she said, walking back into the kitchen. 'I'll do you a back and shoulder massage to help you relax, then we'll get in the Jacuzzi. It's full and the candles are lit. Oh, by the way, the hot tub guy called just after you left – they're bringing it tomorrow.'

'Oh, that's great.' Roy's face brightened. 'We can use it on Saturday night. Perfect! Better tell everyone to bring swim stuff with them.'

'I will. Jane's coming over later with Ed. I've arranged for Claire my beautician to come and do us both a leg and bikini wax. We've no time to go to the salon this week and it's a bit of extra money for Claire. Why don't you and Ed give it a go? Back, sack and crack!'

'What?' He spluttered and almost dropped his coffee mug. 'Sod off, Sam! I'd rather pull my own teeth.'

'Coward,' she said with a laugh. 'You've gone a bit pale.'

'I *feel* pale. Don't know how you can stand that bloody bikini waxing, sets my teeth on edge just thinking about it.'

'It's worth it. And you like the finished effect – I never hear you complaining.'

He smiled. 'I don't care what you look like. I love you just as you are. You know that, but if it makes you happy, go ahead. Not the Brazilian though, it's unfeminine.'

'Even I'm not that brave,' she said with a shudder.

* * *

Sammy poured two large single malts, two glasses of Chardonnay, and an orange juice for the beautician. She grinned to herself as she listened to Jane's shrieks coming from the dining room, which had been turned into a temporary beauty parlour.

She took the single malts up to Roy and Eddie, who were seated with their backs to her, headphones on, singing along to a backing track. She didn't recognise the song, must be one of the new ones for the next album. She liked it though. Nice and upbeat and their harmonies sent a shiver down her spine as always. She set the drinks down on the edge of the mixing desk. Roy turned, winked at her and mouthed, 'Thanks, babe.'

He tapped Eddie on the shoulder and he turned and stuck up a thumb. Roy switched off the deck and they removed their headphones. Eddie grimaced as Jane's yells reached his ears.

'She okay? Sounds like she's being murdered.'

'Just having her bikini line done,' Sammy said. 'Nothing for you to worry about. Normally we go through this agony at the salon. You've no idea the pains we have to endure to look half decent at our age. You two just get up, quick shower, the occasional excuse-for-a-shave, drag a comb through your hair and you're done. Ten minutes, if that, and you still look good. Takes me and Jane at least an hour to get ready and that's just for a bog-standard day. If you're taking us out at night, it's a good half-day session.'

'Yes, but you always look a million dollars to me whether we're going out or staying home,' Roy said.

'Flattery will get you everywhere, Cantello.' She laughed as his dark eyes twinkled with a secret *you-just-wait-until-later* look.

'Right, I'll leave you to it. When Claire goes home, I'll stick some pizzas in the oven and give you a shout. Enjoy your drinks.' She left the room with a spring in her step. How wonderful it felt to be back in her home again and to know that Roy was all hers tonight now that the little ones had gone back to their mother. Could life *be* any better? She'd spoken to Harley earlier and she and Jack were enjoying playing house in the cottage. They were hoping the babies would hit their target weights soon and be allowed home. The excitement in Harley's voice was infectious and brought back to her how thrilled she and Roy had been when they'd first brought Nick home. She'd never forget that long-ago day, or those memories of their first-born that never quite went away.

* * *

Sammy said goodbye to Claire and closed the door behind her. She called Jane to come and join her in the kitchen. 'I'm just going to put the pizzas in,' she said as Jane sat down at the breakfast table.

'So, the hot tub's going out there on the patio?' Jane asked.

'Yeah. We were going to have it on the deck outside the conservatory, but if people want the loo, they'll be traipsing water through the lounge,' Sammy said. 'Be great fun. We'll christen it on Saturday night.'

'Look forward to it.' Jane smiled. 'Bet you can't believe you're back home.'

Sammy shook her head as she took the wrappings off two large pizzas and put them in the oven. She topped up their wine glasses and sat down opposite Jane. 'It's like a dream come true, Jane. I knew he was up to something, but I hadn't a clue what. He was all secretive and kept disappearing and I thought... well, you can guess what I thought.

'Livvy? He wouldn't. You know that. He's absolutely committed to you, Sam. There's no way he'll stray again.'

Sammy chewed her lip and thought about the gold stud that she'd tried to blank from her mind. She still couldn't bring herself to say anything to Roy. His very actions, the way he was with her, wouldn't allow her to believe there was anything going on. But where had it come from? How had it got from Livvy's earlobe to their bedroom carpet?

'What's wrong? You've gone all quiet.'

Sammy looked up and shrugged. 'If I run something by you, will you give me your honest opinion but not say anything to Ed and Roy?'

'Of course. Us Mersey Square girls always stick together.' Jane took a sip of her wine, looking puzzled.

Sammy got up and brought her handbag into the kitchen. She rummaged to the bottom and put the stud on the table.

Jane frowned. 'Isn't that Livvy's? It's like the ones Harley and Jack bought her—'

'Last Christmas,' Sammy finished for her. 'Yes, I think it's Livvy's too.'

'Why have you got it then?'

'Our cleaner picked it up off our bedroom carpet at the cottage last week.'

'What? But what the heck was it doing in your bedroom?'

Sammy looked up at the ceiling for a long moment to compose herself. 'That's the very same question I've asked myself.'

'Does Roy know?'

She shook her head. 'I can't bring myself to ask him. I feel sick when I think about it. I guess it's easier just to block it and see what happens. I'm wondering if something's still going on. He told me earlier that he doesn't want to go over to Ashlea Grange alone again – he said she was all tarted up and he thinks she did that for his benefit. Hank's away so it wasn't for him. But why would she do that unless she thinks she's in with a chance? Has he been giving her the come on?'

'No way!' Jane looked stunned. 'For weeks he's been so excited about this place. He's talked about nothing else but seeing your face when he surprised you. All Roy wants is to make things up to you and he said he'd never stop trying. He was so thrilled when the house came on the market. Why on earth would he jeopardise things now? I don't know how the hell that stud got into your bedroom but I'm damn sure it's not because Roy's had her in your bed. You have to tell him.'

Sammy's eyes filled with tears. 'I can't – I'm too scared in case he tells me he has. God, I hate that bitch! I wish she'd burn in hell.'

'He hasn't, Sam. I'd bet my life on it. There has to be another reason. I don't know what at the moment, but there's no way it's what you're thinking. Get that wine down you, wipe your eyes. I'll get the pizzas out and you give the lads a shout.'

11

'Okay, boys, we're off to see Granny and Grandpa,' Livvy said as she helped Danny and RJ into the car.

'Is Daddy coming too?' RJ asked, wriggling as she struggled to fasten the clasp on his car seat.

'No, he's not. Sit still, please.'

RJ continued to fidget and she slapped his legs and then immediately felt bad as he screamed and kicked out at her, knocking her thumb back.

'Want Daddy!' he howled.

'Shut up, you naughty boy! You've hurt Mummy's hand now and she's got to drive a long way. Here, have your bunny and a sweetie.' She managed to get the clasp fastened while he was distracted and stood back as he fixed her with a malevolent glare from beneath his dark fringe.

'Want Daddy!' he shouted again, pouting. He threw his bunny and the sweetie at her.

She sighed, slammed the door and went round to the other side to fasten Danny in. 'See, Danny's being such a good boy. Why can't you be a good boy too, RJ?' She shook her head and got into the driver's seat. *She* was tired, *they* were tired. RJ had been up half the night crying and Danny had wet the bed. Hopefully they'd fall asleep before too long and she could do the bulk of the journey in peace. She had a banging head that paracetamol hadn't touched and wasn't sure if it was the after-effects of the bump or the copious amount of vodka and Coke she'd consumed last night in an effort to blot out the thoughts of Roy and Sammy together. She'd spoken to Hank before falling asleep and told him that Roy had relented and given her the passports so she'd be joining him later in the week. He'd been overjoyed, said he was really missing her and that he was looking forward to the boys meeting his little grandchildren and what a great family time they'd all have.

She started up the engine and pulled out onto the lane as RJ began shouting again and kicking the back of her seat. He was a nightmare and right at this moment she felt like taking him straight back to Jasmine House and handing him over for good. But that wouldn't do; she wasn't giving in. She turned on the radio, and ignoring the commotion in the back, headed for the M60.

* * *

Sammy took mugs of tea out to the two men who were installing the hot tub and placed them on the picnic table. 'At least the weather's decent,' she said, shading her eyes from the bright sun.

'Yep,' the tallest of the pair agreed.

'I'll leave you to it then. If you need the loo, there's a cloak-room in the hall. Feel free to use it. I'll be unpacking boxes in the house if you want me.' She went back inside, where Roy was reading a newspaper at the breakfast table. 'Bacon butty?' she offered.

'Ah, you know the way to my heart,' he said and tapped her

playfully on the backside. 'With brown sauce,' he added. He folded his paper and went outside for a cigarette.

Sammy smiled as she heard him talking music with the hot-tub guys. They'd never be finished if she didn't get him out of the way. She trimmed fat off several rashers of bacon and popped them under the grill. The phone rang out, making her jump.

'Jane! You're up early. What's up?'

'Not much. I've been thinking about that earring stud. Can you talk?'

'Er, not really.' Sammy lowered her voice. 'Roy's just outside with the workmen. Why don't you come over later when he and Ed are at yours? Bring Pat with you. She and Tim are back from holiday and she's not seen the house yet. I'll do us afternoon tea. Three heads might come up with a solution, although God knows what.'

'That'll be nice. I'll let you put Pat in the picture, see what her reaction is. She knew about the house, by the way.'

Sammy smiled. 'Seems everyone did, but me.'

'Well, that was the idea: a surprise.' Jane laughed. 'See you later then.'

Livvy breathed a sigh of relief as she pulled up outside the detached sandstone bungalow with neat gardens and a white-painted gate. Her dad had been busy by the looks of things. Colourful spring pansies spilled from wicker baskets that hung each side of the door. The hedge was neatly trimmed, lawns freshly mown and the flowerbeds full but tidy, promising future floral displays. Her parents certainly loved their garden. Good job the bad back that she'd told Roy prevented her dad from travelling at the moment wasn't true. He'd had problems a few years ago that had forced him to give up his job, but thanks to her generosity, and a skilled physiotherapist, he'd made a good recovery and was now fit and able. She'd bought her parents the bungalow for their first wedding anniversary.

The front door flew open and Peter, her tall, ginger-haired father, came outside followed by Gina, her petite, blonde-haired mother. Livvy jumped out of the car and the three embraced, all laughing and talking at once.

Gina peeped into the car at her sleeping grandsons: 'Oh, bless them! Little angels.'

'You won't be saying that tonight, Mom, when they won't go to bed. This is their second sleep today. They had a very early start and dropped off before I even got on the motorway. I woke them for breakfast at Tebay Services and they went straight back to sleep as soon as I set off.'

'Well, let's get them inside and then we can catch up. They can lie each end of the sofa for now,' Peter said. 'You girls go inside and I'll carry them in one at a time and then bring your cases in.'

Livvy followed her mother into the bungalow and through to the kitchen that overlooked the back garden. She smiled as she spotted a large garden shed, this year's birthday present to her dad, down near the bottom fence. 'I see he's got it all set up then.'

'Oh, he's never out of it,' Gina said, smiling. 'Best present you could have given him. Wait till he shows you around. He's got it like a wee palace – comfy chairs, kettle and a fridge. Sit down, sweetie. You look tired. I'll make some tea.'

Livvy took a seat on a bar stool while Gina busied herself. They were joined by Peter, who pulled Livvy to her feet and gave her another hug.

'The boys are settled on the sofa. It's so good to see you, hen. Been too long.'

'Good to see you too, Dad. I was just admiring your shed. How are you both? You actually look really well.'

'The tan's left over from our trip to Spain last month,' Gina said, holding out an arm. 'It's fading now. Still, we've got another holiday to Zante booked for June so that's something to look forward to and next week but one we're coming down to see Harley and the new babies. I can't wait. I hope you've brought some photos with you. I can't believe we're great-grand-parents – that's usually a title for really old people with wrin-kles and grey hair!'

Livvy laughed and looked at her very youthful mother, who wasn't even sixty for a couple more years but could easily pass for forty. Her mum and dad had only rediscovered each other in 2001 when she'd made an effort to find them. They'd been teenage sweethearts, but had been separated by angry parents when Gina became pregnant at just fifteen. She was sent to a mother and baby home and Peter had been forbidden to make contact. Livvy had been given away to adoptive parents at six weeks old and Gina taken to live in Canada by her family, while Peter remained in Glasgow. But the pair had never forgotten each other. When Livvy reunited them, they'd fallen in love again and married the following year at the triple ceremony when Harley married Jack and Livvy should have married Roy.

'So, the rest of my family, how are they?' Livvy asked, pushing the sudden thoughts of Roy out of her mind and accepting a mug of tea from Gina.

'Everybody's fine,' Gina said. 'They're all coming over for a barbecue later, Leanne and Pete and their broods. They can't wait to see you and the boys.' Leanne and Pete were the chil-dren from Peter's first marriage and were Livvy's younger half-siblings.

'So anyway,' her dad began, 'this new husband of yours, you say it's Hank, your drummer? Isn't he a little old for you, love?'

Livvy shrugged. 'He's only a couple of years older than Roy. He's a good man, Dad. He loves me very much and looks after me, you know, just like you look after Mom.'

'I'm sure he does,' Gina said. 'But he's older than your dad and it kind of worries us that you only go for older men. We wonder if it's because you're searching for a father figure. We feel it's our fault because we had to give you away and you missed out on a real dad.'

'Oh, Mom! No, you mustn't think like that. It's just a coincidence that Hank's older than me. He was widowed a couple of years ago and we just grew very close. I suppose it was inevitable that we'd marry.'

'Do you love him?' Gina asked.

'I'm very fond of him,' Livvy replied, staring into her mug.

'And is fond enough?' Peter asked, frowning.

'It'll have to be. I'm going to make it work, no matter what.'

'And Roy, how do you feel about him these days?' Gina took hold of Livvy's hand and squeezed it. 'I know you're still hurting, I can see it in your eyes.'

'He was the love of my life but it's well and truly over,' she replied. 'I told you that he married Sammy again. Well, they've just moved back into their old home and they're after full custody of my boys.' She went on to tell them what was happening with the custody battle and Hank wanting them all to live in LA.

Peter shook his head. 'I can't say that I blame Roy, love. Taking his kids away... well, it just isn't on. You have to try and talk Hank into living with you in the UK. Why should you be the one to uproot? Sounds like all of Hank's children are grown up anyway. It's not like he's still got wee ones at home like you. And you've just got new grandchildren. Harley will be so upset if you go and live in the States.' He looked at Gina, whose eyes were filling. 'And so will me and your mother.'

Livvy sighed. 'We've gone over this again and again. Hank's not for bending. Our group is US-based. It's only me that lives over here. I haven't got a choice if I want my marriage to work and to keep singing with Juice.' She stopped as the door pushed open and Danny came into the kitchen, rubbing his eyes. He looked with bewilderment from Peter to Gina and finally to Livvy: 'Oh, did you wonder where you were? Come to Mommy, sweetie. Is RJ still sleeping?'

Danny nodded and ran towards her. She picked him up and cuddled him. 'Say hello to Granny and Grandpa, Danny.'

He smiled and plugged his thumb into his mouth.

'Bless him, he's shy,' Gina said and ran her fingers through his blond curls. 'He looks more like you these days than he does Daniel. I can see Courtney in him too. RJ looks more like Roy and Harley than ever.'

'The devil child,' Livvy muttered as Gina raised an eyebrow. 'He's such hard work at the moment. I hope he improves when he turns three. Terrible twos isn't in it with that one! He's apparently as good as gold for Roy and Sammy and a monkey for me.'

'It'll get easier when he's a few months older,' Gina said.

'Let's hope so.' Livvy rolled her eyes. 'Are you still okay to babysit tomorrow while I have a night out with Sheena? We've a lot of catching up to do. I told you I'm off to LA on Thursday, didn't I? So I've only got the one night to see her. I want to spend tonight with my family here.'

'Of course, it'll be our pleasure,' Peter said. 'Sounds like you need a break from the wee ones too. Do you good to have a girls' night out.'

* * *

'So, what do you think?' Jane asked as she, Sammy and Pat relaxed in the lounge at Jasmine House. They'd just stuffed themselves with scones, jam, clotted cream and Earl Grey tea and Sammy had insisted on a glass of champagne to finish. She'd related the tale of the gold stud to Pat.

'Well, like you and Sam, I haven't a clue,' Pat said. 'I mean, why the heck would Roy jeopardise everything you've built up again for a quickie with Livvy? It doesn't make sense. And like Jane said, he's been so chuffed about getting the house back for you. It's like the ultimate gift. There's no way it's what you're thinking, Sam. I mean, could she have lent the studs to Harley?'

'I'd considered that but I doubt it,' Sammy said. 'They're not the sort of thing Harley wears. She's like me, prefers danglies. And I'm sure if she'd borrowed them and lost one she'd have said something and had the house tipped upside down looking for it. Besides, Harley never really goes into our bedroom and she was in hospital that week. It couldn't have been there long because Mrs Melcher would have seen it, or me, or one of us might even have stood on it with a bare foot. I'm at a loss. I can't put it out of my mind and I know I'll have to ask him or it'll eat away at me. Once we get this weekend and the house-warming out of the way, I'll tackle him about it.'

* * *

'I got married the other week to Hank, my drummer,' Livvy announced quietly, picking up her glass of wine. She sat back as Sheena's mouth fell open, her green eyes registering shock. They were seated in a small, intimately lit alcove in up-market St Jude's Restaurant, waiting for starters. Livvy was conscious of people staring in her direction and whispering behind hands. She wished the waiter had seated them a bit more discreetly, but they'd been lucky to get a table at such short notice. She'd kidded herself no one would recognise her and kept her eyes focused firmly on her old school friend.

'Married?' Sheena stared at her. 'Oh my God! Why didn't you tell me?'

'Shhh! I was saving it as a surprise. Not even the press knows yet. No one knows except family and a few others.'

'Well, bloody hell, Liv, it's a surprise alright! I'm gobsmacked. And he's so much older than you.' She lowered her voice. 'Can he still... you know?'

In spite of trying not to attract attention, Livvy laughed. Trust Sheena. 'Of course he can,' she whispered. 'You never asked me that about Roy. Hank's only two years older.'

'Well, let's face it, I didn't *need* to ask you that about Roy – Mr-sex-on-legs!' Sheena smirked as Livvy felt her cheeks warming. 'I can't believe it, I thought you'd never get married after the fiasco with Roy. It would have put me off forever. I presume he knows? What did he say?'

'He wished us well. Didn't seem in the least bit bothered. I don't want to spend the rest of my life on my own,' Livvy said. 'The boys need a father figure.'

'Well, they've got Roy. You told me they spend loads of time with him.'

'They do and he's a great father, loves them to bits. But they need someone in the home too. Hank's really good with them. I'm struggling to cope on my own. RJ's hard work.' She brought Sheena up to speed with all her news and waited for a response, which was no surprise when it came.

'LA? For good? I don't think you'll win that one, Liv. Roy's high-profile, more so than you are over here. He'll use his fame to gain public sympathy.'

Livvy shook her head. 'He won't. He doesn't court publicity, never has done. I just don't know what to do. I mean, Danny's my son, he's not even Roy's flesh and blood, but he's brought him up and his name's on the birth certificate. He's Danny Cantello and obviously that gives Roy as many rights as I've got. I've even toyed with the idea of leaving RJ with Roy and taking Danny with me but it wouldn't be fair to split them up.'

'Oh no, that's something you can't do,' Sheena agreed. 'It would be too cruel. Persuade Hank to live over here, that'll solve everything.'

Livvy sighed. *Here we go again. Everybody thought the same thing. Why couldn't Hank see it'd be the easiest option all round?* 'He won't,' she said. 'And Roy refuses to let me take the boys out of the country. He doesn't know I'm going to LA with them, he thinks I'm staying up here for the next few days. I, erm, I borrowed their passports without his knowledge.' She told Sheena how she'd managed to get the passports from the cottage.

'Wow, you don't half surprise me sometimes! You used to be such a wee mouse. You're taking a hell of a gamble. If Roy finds out, you'll lose your boys for sure.'

'It's a chance I have to take. Hopefully I'll get away with it. But next time we go, it'll be for good. I'll just have to disappear while the dust settles. I trust you not to tell anyone, Sheena. I've no one else to talk to and I can't tell my parents as they'd go mad.'

Sheena shook her head. She patted Livvy's hand. 'I won't say a word but I don't approve. Just so you know,' she added as the waiter brought two dishes of sizzling garlic prawns to the table.

'Mmm, thank you,' Sheena said. 'Smells wonderful. I don't really know what the answer is, Liv. I guess there isn't one. Put it out of your head for now and let's have a good night. You need to relax. There's live music in the bar later. We'll have a dance and you can tell me how Jon Mellor's coping with being a grandpa.'

Livvy smiled. 'Did he not call you and tell you himself?'

Sheena screwed up her nose. 'I got a text after *you* told me the news. Brief and to the point: "*Twins – one of each. Harley and babies doing well.*" He doesn't keep in touch on a regular basis. No point. It was just a fling, an afternoon of madness. He's in love with Jess and it shouldn't have happened, he told me. I've put it behind me and I guess he has too.'

Livvy raised an eyebrow. 'These things have a habit of

catching up with you when you least expect it.' Sheena's very
brief fling with Jess Mellor's husband Jon had been over before
it began and would hopefully stay buried in memory. With a bit
of luck, Jess and Sheena's husband, Gerry, would be none the
wiser.

* * *

'I'll call you tomorrow, Dad.' Livvy hugged her father goodbye
and turned to kiss her mother, who was tearfully cuddling her
grandsons and making RJ promise to be a very good boy for
Mommy on the plane. He nodded solemnly, then turned and
pushed Danny over.

'See what I mean?' Livvy said. 'One minute an angel, next a
wee so-and-so!' She picked Danny up and he snuggled into her
neck, crying, while her mother grabbed hold of RJ, who tried to
run away. He screamed at the top of his voice, attracting attention that Livvy really didn't need. She'd scraped her distinctive
blonde curls into a topknot, squashed a baseball cap over it and
was hiding behind a pair of over-large shades. The last thing she
needed was a snap-happy paparazzi lurking, or Roy would
know tomorrow that she'd taken the boys out of the country.
She was conscious of her mum speaking and turned her attention back.

'I think RJ's jealous,' Gina said.

'But why? He gets as much attention as Danny, if not more.'

'Well, we're always saying what a good boy Danny is and
how naughty RJ is. He was okay last night when we looked after
him, not a scrap of trouble. You need to praise him a bit more.
Maybe you're expecting too much from him – he's not even
three yet.'

Livvy sighed. 'Maybe I am. I'm not used to kids. Roy
brought Harley up, the housekeeper and Daniel raised
Courtney for much of her young life while I was on tour and I

had Roy around to help me with Danny's first few months. It all went pear-shaped when he left me alone and pregnant with him.' She nodded in RJ's direction.

'Do you think maybe you resent RJ a little?' Gina asked. 'You know, because Roy's not with you, I mean. You told me he's more than pulled his weight with them, both he and Sammy. So you get lots of free time. More than most mothers do. But RJ's so like Roy that maybe he's too much of a reminder.'

'Oh, I don't know.' Livvy shook her head. 'Maybe. But whatever, I'm not looking forward to the next few hours. Hopefully they'll sleep for most of it.'

'Well, you're in first class so you should be able to spread out a bit,' Peter said. 'I think you'd better go through, hen, they're calling passengers for your flight. They'll let you on first with the wee ones. Good luck, we'll talk to you tomorrow.' He gave her a kiss and a hug.

'Thanks, Dad. See you soon. Bye, Mom, love you both.'

'We love you too, sweetie,' Gina said, hugging and kissing her. 'Safe journey. We'll pick you up next week and then you can have another night with us before you drive home.'

12

Harley struggled into her new slim-fitting dress, smoothing down the blue silk fabric over her stomach. She turned sideways in front of the mirror and pulled in her middle. 'It's no use, Jack. I can't wear this, I still look pregnant. You won't even be able to do up the zip, never mind undo it later.' She sighed. So much for the bit of passion they'd planned to have after the party. Jack wouldn't fancy her, all flabby and wobbly-bellied like this, not to mention her droopy boobs. She'd be lucky if she ever looked normal again.

Jack came up behind her, slipped his arms around her waist and nuzzled her neck. 'You look just fine to me.' He rubbed both hands over her stomach, spun her around and kissed her. 'You look wonderful, Harley. You always do.'

She sighed and snuggled closer. 'I feel such a mess. I'm fat and my boobs are still leaking. I so wanted to look nice for you tonight.' A tear slid down her cheek and Jack brushed it away.

'Wear the outfit your mum bought you. It's loose and you might feel better about yourself. You can always wear the dress when your tummy goes down.'

Harley stiffened in his arms. 'So you *do* think I look fat?'

Jack bit his lip. 'I didn't mean it like that. You know I didn't. You've just had two babies, it takes time for everything to go back into place. They told you that. You shouldn't be squeezing into tight things, you need to feel comfortable.'

Harley reached in the wardrobe and took out the loose cotton pants and floaty top that her mum had treated her to yesterday. A pale-coffee shade with gold trim; the colour complemented her long dark hair and brown eyes perfectly. 'Okay, I'll wear these and some gold jewellery. See if you can find my gold, strappy sandals, Jack. They're probably at the bottom of the wardrobe.'

* * *

'You okay, Roy?' Sammy asked as she joined him on the patio, where he was organising the hired tables and chairs. He had his phone in his hand and a frown on his face.

'Just been trying to call Livvy. That's three times I've rung her in the last couple of days and she hasn't picked up or replied to my texts. I need to know if the boys are okay, that's all.'

Sammy raised an eyebrow and walked over to a pair of trestle tables. She threw white cloths over them and began folding gold-coloured paper napkins. Was he really calling Livvy to ask about the boys, or simply to hear her voice? She shook her head. *Stop thinking like that. He wouldn't. Please, let's have a Livvy-free night.* She fixed on a bright smile. 'You know, love,' she began, talking to his back as he tightened the legs on a table, 'you constantly calling could just be annoying her. Maybe she's not answering on purpose. *You* always hate it when she calls you and asks if they're okay. You tell her to stop interfering.'

He turned and frowned. 'I'm showing fatherly concern, that's all. It's not like they're around the corner, she's taken them bloody miles away.' He stopped as a small girl, shrieking

'Grandpa!', hurtled through the patio doors and wrapped her arms around his legs. She was followed by Jason and Jules, their arms full of flowers and packages.

Roy swung the little girl into the air before sitting her on his shoulders. Sammy smiled. Thank God for that. Their four-year-old granddaughter Daisy could wrap him round her little finger. He ran around the patio with her, swaying from side to side so that she giggled and held onto his ears, her long dark hair flying out behind. He lifted her down and she smoothed out the skirt of her pink sparkly party dress and did a twirl.

'Do I look pretty?' she said, squealing again as he grabbed her and tickled her ribs.

'Pretty? Daisy, you look like a princess,' he told her.

'Where are Danny and RJ?' Daisy asked, looking around.

'They're not here, sweetheart,' Sammy said. 'They've gone to see their granny and grandpa in Scotland.'

Daisy pouted and stuck her hands on her hips. 'I wanted to play with them.'

'I'm sorry, love. You can come for tea and a sleepover next week when they're home. Here, come and help me with a very important job.' Sammy pulled up a chair so that Daisy could reach the table. 'I need the napkins folding into triangles. Do you think you can manage that all on your own while I go indoors for something?'

Daisy nodded importantly, climbed onto the chair and took over the napkin folding.

'Well done, Mum,' Jason said and followed her back inside.

'It'll keep her occupied for a while,' Sammy said, lifting trays of marinated steaks and chicken breasts out of the fridge.

Jason placed a crate of assorted wines on the worktop and handed a colourful, elaborately arranged bunch of gerberas, tied up with a cream raffia bow, to his mum: 'For you. How are you settling in?'

'Thank you, darling. They're beautiful.' She gave Jason a

hug. 'We're settling in just fine. It feels like we've never lived anywhere else. Your dad's a bit cat-on-hot-bricks tonight though, so go easy with him.'

'Why?' Jason frowned, putting the white wines in the fridge. 'He seemed fine just now with Daisy.'

'He can't get hold of Livvy. She's not picking up his calls so he's a bit annoyed.'

'He'll be alright when he's had a few single malts,' Jason said. 'Shall I take one out to him and get Jules a glass of red wine while I'm at it?'

'Please, love. Pour me a red as well and help yourself to whatever you want.'

As Jason left the kitchen, the front door opened and Sammy heard a shout of, 'It's only us.' She looked up to see Harley and Jack.

'Oh, you look lovely, sweetheart,' Sammy said, throwing her arms around Harley.

'Thanks, Mum. But you don't have to be kind. I know I look horrible.'

'You look stunning, you silly girl. You really do. Your hair looks lovely. All the shine's coming back to it. I told you it would once the babies arrived.' Harley's hair hung dark and glossy past her shoulders and her carefully made-up face complemented her new outfit.

'Doesn't she?' Jack agreed. 'She won't have it, thinks she's fat. I'll take our case up to the guest room.'

'I'm glad you're staying over,' Sammy said. 'We can have a girlie morning tomorrow 'cos no doubt our menfolk will want a long lie-in.'

Harley nodded. 'You can come over to the hospital with me while I feed the babies if you like. In fact, you can feed one yourself.'

'Oh yes, please,' Sammy said. 'That will be wonderful, love. Any news on them coming home yet?'

'About Wednesday, all being well. They said possibly midweek anyway. I'm so excited, Mum.'

'Me too, darling.' Sammy gave her a hug. 'Your dad's outside with Jules, Jason and Daisy. Go and join them and get a soft drink. There's plenty of choice because I know you can't have alcohol while you're still giving the babies your own milk. Give Daisy a drink while you're at it – her princess cup's in the cupboard near the door.'

'What a shame the boys aren't here,' Harley said. 'Daisy's got no one to play with.'

'She's got your father,' Sammy said dryly 'She'll have him hula-hooping when he's had a few. He reverts to second childhood when she's around. Did you bring your swim things for the hot tub?'

'No.' Harley shook her head. 'Jack did, but I can't get in with my leaky boobs. I'll have to try it another time.'

The intercom for the gates buzzed as Harley went outside. Sammy let in her guests and opened the front door to greet Eddie and Jane, and Phil Jackson, The Raiders' rhythm guitarist, and his wife Laura, who'd arrived in convoy. She welcomed them all with hugs and kisses.

'Jess and Jon are on their way with Kate and Zak,' Jane said. She and Eddie's youngest daughter Kate was married to Phil's son, Zak.

'Come on through to the patio,' Sammy said as the buzzer went again. 'Just help yourselves to drinks while I let them in.'

Jess, Jon, Kate and Zak handed Sammy a large bunch of yellow roses and bottles of wine.

'You didn't need to bring any wine. There's plenty, but thanks anyway, and the roses are beautiful,' she said. 'Nearly all here now. Just waiting for Pat and Tim and Sean and Tina; Carl and Cathy can't make it.'

'Nor can Nathan,' Jess said of Jack's twin brother. 'He's tied up in London. Jack was hoping he'd be back in time, but there you go. Are Harley and Jack here?'

'Yes. Harley's outside... oh, and here's Jack now,' Sammy said as Jack ran down the stairs.

'Been hanging Harley's clothes up,' Jack said, greeting his parents and grandparents with hugs.

'She's got *you* well-trained, son,' Jon said, ruffling Jack's unruly mop of dark curls that resembled his own.

Jack smiled good-naturedly. 'I don't mind, she's worth it.'

'Hmm, you say that now, but just you wait!'

'Hey, you!' Jess smacked Jon on the arm. 'Come on, let's go and find a drink. I need one, been a busy day.'

'Shopping, having your hair and nails done and lunch out with Mum,' Jon teased. 'Very busy, Jess. But you look fabulous,' he added, 'so it was worth it.' He pulled her close and planted a kiss on her lips.

'Dad!' Jack said, rolling his eyes. 'Do me a favour.'

'You won't be saying that when you're our age,' Jon said. 'Right, lead the way. There must be a bottle of lager in the fridge with my name on it.'

* * *

Livvy rolled over and looked at her phone, buzzing on the bedside table. Roy – again. She could hear shrieks and splashing from outside the bedroom window and smiled. Hank and the boys were in the pool while she was having a morning in bed. They'd had such a busy previous day and late night with birthday celebrations for Hank's daughter and then the boys had been wired from sugary drinks and candies and so hard to settle. She'd spent hours reading to them and this morning, when they'd come running into the bedroom and jumped on the bed, Hank had insisted she stay where she was and he'd take charge. He'd brought her pancakes and coffee and then left her to a much-needed sleep – he was so good with the boys.

This was what they all needed, a man around to help and to look after her, too. When she'd finally managed to crawl into bed, he'd taken her in his arms and held her close, telling her how much he loved and needed her and she found herself responding in a way she hadn't before. They made love with more passion than she'd ever thought possible. Maybe it was alcohol that loosened her inhibitions, but something deep within her had come back to life and she liked it. She stretched and sighed, wishing that he was here beside her now. Maybe the boys would have an afternoon nap and Hank would join her. She felt a bit guilty at not answering Roy's calls but was terrified that he might realise she wasn't in Glasgow. She certainly couldn't call him back because her call might register International on his caller display. He'd just have to wait until the following week. The boys were fine and if there was an emergency then she'd have to call him, but for now... she simply couldn't be bothered. Roy had got what he wanted, Sammy back and his old home. Why should he have all the fun? It was time for her to enjoy some happiness of her own with Hank.

* * *

'Would you like me to come and stay for a few days next week?' Jess said to Harley. 'You'll need an extra pair of hands on site to help with the babies, so that you and Jack can have a bit of time to yourselves now and again.'

'That's if we get them home,' Harley said. 'But yes, please, Jess. I'll take as much help as I can get. No doubt Mum and Jane will want to do their bit too.'

'What about Livvy? When will she be back from visiting her parents? It seems so weird, sharing grandchildren with her.'

'Bet it seems weird sharing them with Dad when he's old

enough to be their great-grandpa, like Uncle Ed,' Harley said, laughing. 'Mom's home on Tuesday. What a crazy mixed-up family we are.'

'Hmm,' Sammy said, joining them on the patio. 'Well, we know who we've got to thank for that.' She looked pointedly at Roy, who was seated in the hot tub in animated conversation about The Raiders' next album with Eddie, Tim and Phil. 'Talk about lads' night out! They can have ten more minutes and then it's our turn, girls.'

Daisy, sucking her thumb, came to sit on Sammy's knee. 'Are you tired, sweetheart?' Sammy asked, pushing Daisy's hair out of her eyes.

Daisy shook her head. 'Grandpa won't come on the trampoline with me.'

Jess grinned. 'Now that I'd like to see!'

'He said he's too old,' Daisy continued. 'Will you come, Granny, please?'

'Erm, I'm not sure that's a good idea, Daisy.' Sammy squeezed her and gave her a kiss. 'I think I'm too old to be jumping around on a trampoline, too.'

'Auntie Harley, will you?' Daisy stuck her bottom lip out.

'I can't, darling, I've just had the babies,' Harley said, placing her hands over her chest. 'But I tell you what – Granny and Jess are waiting their turn to go in the hot tub, so why don't I play hula-hoop with you?'

Daisy's face brightened. 'Okay.' She scrambled down off Sammy's knee. 'I'll go and find two. Would you like a pink one or a purple one?'

'I don't mind, but I'm just going to pop to the loo first.' Harley got to her feet and went indoors.

'Shall we girls get changed and chuck that lot out?' Jess said. 'They've had long enough.'

'Use the spare room, Jess. I'll go and hurry them along.'

Sammy handed out towels as the reluctant men climbed out of the tub.

'You should have joined us, Sammy,' Jon said, wrapping a towel around his waist.

'That was the plan,' Sammy said. 'Mixed sessions, but you lot took over. Anyway, we're getting in now and you can wait on us. Make sure you keep our glasses filled.'

'We'll do better than that,' Roy said, pulling her close. 'We'll serenade you. We're going to have a bit of a jam out here, play you some of the new album while you relax. You can give us your first impressions.'

Sammy smiled. 'The song you were playing the other night with Ed was great. Just like old Raiders' stuff.'

'That's what we're aiming for,' Eddie said. 'A back-to-our-roots album, like the rockers we used to be. A sort of we're-not-going-away feel.'

'That's it,' Phil said. 'A great name for the album, "Not Fade Away". Perfect.'

'Excellent, Phil,' Roy said. 'We'll include the track,' he added as Eddie and Tim nodded their approval.

'Sammy,' Jess called from the patio doors and beckoned.

'What is it?' she asked, going to Jess's side.

'Harley's still in the cloakroom. Daisy was knocking on the door, hula-hoops in hand. She said Auntie Harley was still in there but wouldn't talk to her.'

'Oh my God!' Sammy rushed inside and banged on the cloakroom door. 'Are you sure she's not gone upstairs?' she said to Jess. 'Go and have a look in case she's having a lie-down.' Jess dashed off and Sammy banged on the door again: 'Harley, Harley, love, it's Mum, are you okay?' She looked at Daisy's worried little face. 'Daisy, go and get Grandpa and Uncle Jack, please. There's a good girl.'

Jess came rushing back downstairs. 'She's not up there. Oh hell, I hope she's okay.'

Roy and Jack came into the hall, towels wrapped around their middles.

'What's wrong?' Roy asked.

'Harley's been in there ages and she's not answering,' Sammy said. 'You need to break the door down but be careful, she may be lying behind it.'

Jason appeared carrying Daisy. 'Take her back outside, love,' Sammy whispered. 'Something's happened to Harley, your dad's going to break the door down.'

Roy put his shoulder to the door and pushed. It creaked but didn't open. He tried again and the door gave way. Harley lay on the floor, deathly white, and her eyes staring. He dropped to his knees and cradled her, while Jack frantically shouted her name.

'She's still breathing, thank God,' Roy said. 'Get a blanket and call an ambulance, quick!'

13

As the paramedics helped Harley into the ambulance, Roy organised transport to the hospital. Jack, still wearing swimming shorts with a towel around his middle, was allowed to travel with her. Sammy thrust his clothes at him.

'Get dressed on the way and we'll be with you as soon as we can,' she said and watched the blue lights flashing as the vehicle sped away down the drive. She dashed back indoors and ran into Roy and Jason, who was the only one not drinking.

'Jason's taking us to the hospital,' Roy told her. 'The others will stay on here until we know what's wrong.'

'Okay.' Sammy held him close. She felt him shaking and he was as white as the kitchen tiles; he'd sobered instantly by the events of the last half-hour. She took his hand and led him out to Jason's Range Rover, helped him into the back and climbed up beside him. 'Does Jules know he can put Daisy to bed in the nursery?' she said to Jason, who clambered in and started the engine.

'Yeah, Mum, don't worry, he'll sort it. Did the guys say what's happened?'

'No, but she was making noises as they lifted her onto the stretcher,' Sammy replied. 'Coming round a little, I think.'

'Do you think it's a fit or something?' Roy asked, his voice wobbling. 'I can't bear this. She's gone through so much in the last few years, she doesn't deserve anything else to cope with.'

'I don't know, love. She seemed fine earlier – blooming, in fact – and everyone was saying how well she looked.'

'Then it can't be anything serious, can it?' His voice held a pleading note. 'Maybe she just fainted. Perhaps she banged her head and it knocked her for six.'

She rubbed his arm, not daring to voice her thoughts. Harley's eyes had looked vacant, staring into space as though seeing nothing.

'Let's wait until we get there. Only a few minutes now.'

Jack was waiting for them in the corridor as they dashed inside. He led them to a small waiting room, where he'd been told to stay until called. Sammy pulled him into her arms and he sobbed against her. 'Have they given you any idea of what's wrong?' she asked, sitting him down and taking the seat next to him.

He shook his head, sniffing. Sammy dug in her pocket and handed him a tissue. 'She was trying to say something but they put a mask over her face.'

'Well, at least she was trying to communicate,' Roy said, sitting down on the other side of Jack. 'That's something.'

They sat in silence for what felt like hours. Jason went to find a coffee machine. Eventually, a serious-faced young doctor, clutching a file, came in to see them. He introduced himself and sat down opposite. Jack got to his feet and Sammy moved up next to Roy.

'What's the score?' Roy asked and grabbed Sammy's hand.

'We've taken Harley back to Maternity for now until we get some more results in. I'm afraid it's possible she's suffered a CVT – a cerebral venous thrombosis.'

'A what?' Roy said as Sammy took a deep breath.

'A stroke, a post-partum stroke. It sometimes happens when a mother has had complications like pre-eclampsia during pregnancy. Harley has a blood clot, which has led to a clot developing in a vein to her brain.'

'Bloody hell!' Roy choked, his face a mask of agony. 'A stroke? She's only just twenty. I thought old people got strokes? Is she going to be okay?'

'It's too early to say what the outcome will be. We'll do a full MRI scan tomorrow. She has paralysis to her left side and her speech is slurred, so communication will be difficult for her at the moment. But please remember that she can hear and see all you say and do. Try and remain calm when you're with her. She'll appear confused but can tell what you're saying, she just can't make herself understood. Maternity are expecting you and provisions have been made for Jack to stay with her. I know it's pointless me saying this, but do try not to worry. While serious, most of the symptoms of this type of stroke are reversible, given time. I'll speak with you tomorrow, Mr Cantello, and hopefully, we'll have confirmation of her condition.'

The doctor left the room and Jack fell back into Sammy's arms while Jason held his devastated father close.

'Come on,' Sammy said after a few minutes, 'let's get Jack over to Maternity and you can go in with him, Roy. I doubt they'll let us all in at once. I'll ring home and put Jane in the picture and then she can let everyone know.'

* * *

Jane dropped the phone back onto the kitchen table and went outside to report what Sammy had just told her.

'I'll make us all a coffee,' she said and went back inside, Eddie on her heels.

Jess burst into tears and Jon pulled her to his side. 'Come

on, Jess, Harley's a fighter. Look at everything she's come through in the last few years. She'll pull through this too.'

'But the babies...' Jess cried. 'Poor little things. How can something like this happen to such a lovely young girl – and she was so happy tonight? It's just not fair.'

Jane stood by the sink, her shoulders shaking. Eddie took her in his arms and held her until her tears subsided. 'I can't believe it,' she sobbed. 'Hasn't poor Harley gone through enough? And what about our Jack? He'll be devastated.'

Eddie shook his head. 'It's unbelievable. Are Sammy and Roy staying the night at the hospital?'

'No, but Jack is. They'll be back in a while.' Jane wiped her eyes on a sheet of kitchen roll. 'I'll make that pot of coffee and perhaps you can go and look for brandy. There's a drinks cabinet in the dining room.'

As Eddie left the kitchen, Jane busied herself brewing the coffee and loaded a tray with mugs and a milk jug. No one took sugar but she included a small dish of cubes in case anyone felt they needed it for shock – she felt numb herself. Eddie came back with a bottle of brandy. He handed it to Jane and carried the tray outside. It was still quite warm and Jules had lit the patio heaters.

'Help yourselves,' Jane said. 'Put a nip of brandy in too.' She looked at Tina, Harley's godmother, who was wiping her eyes: 'You okay, Tina?'

Tina nodded and took a gulp of air. 'Has anyone told Livvy?'

'I've no idea,' Jane replied. 'I expect Roy will do that. She's at her parents' place in Glasgow with the boys, so there's nothing she can do tonight anyway. Perhaps she'll drive home tomorrow.'

'She'll be so upset,' Sean, Tina's husband and Harley's godfather, said. 'Hope she'll be okay to drive.'

'Maybe her mum and dad will come back with her and

share the driving,' Jane said. 'Jack said they were due to come and visit soon to see the babies.' She looked up as Sammy, Roy and Jason came out onto the patio. 'Oh, how is she?'

Roy shrugged. 'Comfortable. She's having a scan tomorrow and that will tell them more. Hopefully the damage is mild and she'll make a good recovery. But we've been warned it won't be instant. Jack's in bits, poor lad. What a thing to happen.'

'Tina was wondering if you'd told Livvy,' Jane said.

Roy shook his head and reached for the brandy bottle. He tipped some into an empty glass and knocked it back in one go. 'It's too late to call her now, I'll do it in the morning. She can drive home tomorrow instead of Monday. I'll have to ring her parents' landline if she won't answer. Does anyone have it, by the way?'

'Jack and Harley do,' Sammy said. 'I'll speak to Jack in the morning and find out if he's got it on his phone. If not, I'll nip over to the cottage for their address book. Is everyone staying over?'

'We'll get out from under your feet, Sam,' Tina said. 'You've enough on your plate. We'll call you tomorrow to see how things are. Give Jack and Harley our love when you see them. Sean, ring for a taxi.'

'Book one for us and Phil, too,' Tim said from across the patio, where he sat with his arms around a weeping Pat.

'You sure, mate?' Roy said. 'You're more than welcome to stay.'

'We'll go,' Pat said. 'You really *do* have enough on your hands. Give Harley our love and we'll come over tomorrow.'

'We'll stay,' Eddie said, nodding at Jane.

'And so will we,' Jon added. 'Just in case we're needed for Jack.'

'I'll make some more coffee,' Jane said and took the pot back indoors.

'You okay?' Jane asked, giving Sammy a hug as she came back into the kitchen.

Sammy shook her head. 'I'm numb, I just can't believe it. She's got no use in her left side and Roy said her face is droopy. He said she looks terrified. Poor kid, as if she hasn't had enough.'

Jane nodded. 'Let's have this last drink and then get to bed. We'll need our wits about us tomorrow – Roy looks shattered.'

* * *

'She's still not picking up,' Roy said, flinging his phone onto the kitchen table. 'I can't send her that sort of news in a text, can I?'

'No,' Sammy agreed. 'You need to talk to her. I'll text Jack for her parents' number. Eat some of that toast.' She pushed a plate towards him. 'It's going to be a long day today and you need something inside you to soak up all that alcohol. I'll make a proper breakfast when the others finish in the shower.'

Roy nodded. He'd sat up all night drinking and felt rough, tired and emotionally shattered. He was dreading the phone ringing with any further news but needed to know how Harley was doing. Jack had called first thing to say they were taking her for a scan at nine. How had things got so bad? Surely life couldn't throw anything else at his poor girl? His head was thumping and he felt sick. Coffee and toast might take the edge off.

Jack texted Livvy's parents' number back to Sammy and Roy made one last attempt to call her cell phone. He was about to hang up when the call was answered. He could hear a child's voice, distant, but chattering, and Roy shouted, 'Hello!' He heard giggling and then another child's voice – RJ and Danny must have got hold of her phone. 'RJ, it's Daddy, give the phone to Mommy, please.' The chattering became muffled and intermittent and Roy realised whichever child it was had his hand over the mouthpiece. He tried again: 'Danny give the phone to

Mommy.' Still nothing, then a man's voice, clear this time, saying, 'Boys, it's the middle of the night, you're supposed to be sleeping. You're gonna disturb Mommy. Give me the phone and get back into bed.' Roy frowned as the call disconnected. The voice sounded like Hank's. Middle of the night? Supposed to be sleeping? What the fuck was going on?

'What's wrong, love?' Sammy sat down beside him.

'Somebody just answered the phone. The kids, or at least *a* kid, don't know if it was ours, hard to tell, it was all muffled, and then a guy told them to get back into bed and disconnected. Sounded like Hank.'

'Maybe they're home and she's not letting on because they want the kids for the weekend.'

'No, I heard him say it was the middle of the night. I bet she's left the bloody kids with her parents and gone off to see Hank in LA. That was probably one of his grandchildren got hold of her phone. No wonder she doesn't want to talk to me.'

'Call Peter and Gina then, here's the number.' Sammy handed him the piece of paper she'd scribbled it down on.

He dialled and waited. Peter answered and Roy asked to speak to Livvy.

'She's not here, Roy,' Peter replied. 'She's gone to LA with the wee boys. We're picking her up tomorrow afternoon. Try her cell phone later today if it's urgent.'

'LA?' Roy spluttered. 'Oh, of course. Thank you. Goodbye.' He hung up before Peter could question his call and stared at Sammy.

'What?'

'She's in fucking LA with the kids! That *was* Hank I heard.'

Sammy frowned. 'How has she managed that? No wonder she won't speak to you. Do you think she's bought false passports? What a bitch! Where are you going?' she asked as Roy jumped to his feet, sending his chair flying. She followed him out of the room and up to their bedroom.

He grabbed his old briefcase from the wardrobe and rooted inside, flinging papers all over the floor. 'They're gone! The passports, they're gone!' he yelled as Sammy looked on in bewilderment. 'How the fuck has that happened?'

She shook her head. 'I've no idea. Oh my God, you need to call your solicitor right away!'

'What good will that do?' he shouted. 'She's taken my kids. That's it, she can just vanish on a whim now. I might never get them back. I don't understand how she got her hands on the passports. They've never been out of our sight. How the fuck did she get in our home without our knowledge?' He stopped as Jane and Eddie popped their heads around the door.

'What's wrong?' Eddie asked, stepping into the room, Jane following.

Sammy explained, running her hands through her hair.

'Hell, how's she managed that?' Eddie asked.

'That's what I'd like to know,' Roy shouted, walking up and down agitatedly. 'I can't believe this.'

Jane clapped a hand to her mouth and stared wide-eyed at Sammy.

'The stud! That has to be it.'

'Oh my God!' Sammy exclaimed. 'Jane, you're right.'

Roy looked at them both. 'Stud? What stud? What are you on about?'

Sheepishly, Sammy told him about Mrs Melcher finding Livvy's earring in their bedroom.

'And you never thought to say anything to me?' he said, dark eyes angry.

'I was going to,' she faltered, 'but I thought... well, I thought something might be going on between you and Livvy. I was scared of voicing my concerns.'

Roy took a deep breath. His face paled and he spat his reply: 'After everything we've been to each other for the last few years you didn't trust me enough to ask me? You thought I was screwing her again? Well, that's fucking great, Sam! I've got a critically ill daughter, two kids abducted by their lunatic mother and a wife who doesn't trust me, no matter what I do to try and make things right.' He stormed out of the room and slammed the door so hard, their wedding picture in the alcove fell down, smashing the glass in the frame as Sammy dropped to her knees, sobbing.

14

Eddie found Roy sitting on the patio, smoking and knocking back single malt. He'd left Jane upstairs, comforting a distraught Sammy. 'There you are. Mind if I join you?' He helped himself to a cigarette and a light. Roy pushed the bottle of whisky across the picnic table but Eddie declined: 'Too early for me.'

Roy looked at him, a pained expression in his eyes. 'How could she do that, Ed? Not trust me enough to say something, I mean? After everything we've said and done the last few years and she still doesn't trust me.'

Eddie coughed a cloud of smoke above his head. 'You shouldn't even be asking yourself that, mate. Given your track record with Livvy, what the hell was she supposed to think? Give her a break. She's gutted. Blaming herself for the boys going missing. It's Livvy you should be losing your rag with, not Sammy.'

Roy at least had the grace to look shamefaced. 'Believe me, if I could get hold of her I would. But if Sammy had told me, between us we'd have worked out why the stud was in the bedroom. At least I could have confronted Livvy about it before she took off. What if she doesn't bring my kids back? She might even go on the run with them once she realises I'm on to her. I need to tell her about Harley. I'm gonna have to call her folks again to see if they have a number for Hank.' He knocked back the remains of his drink and got to his feet. 'I'd better go and make my peace with Sam.'

* * *

Jane bent to pick up the broken pieces of glass from behind the door. 'At least your wedding photo's not damaged,' she said to Sammy, who was slumped on the bed, sobbing. Jane looked at the happy couple, all smiles and with their arms around each other. 'The frame's got a bit of a chip in it though.' She put it down on the bedside table and the shards of glass into the wastepaper bin in the bathroom. 'I'll go and make you some tea.'

'What if he never forgives me?' Sammy cried. 'He was in such a state and it's all my fault.'

Jane was at a loss as to what to say and do. She was sure that once Roy got his head together, he'd be back up there and Sammy would be instantly forgiven.

'Please stop it, Sam.' She handed over a box of tissues. 'Of course it's not your fault. Listen, I'd have jumped to the same conclusion, I'm sure.'

'No, you wouldn't. You said it couldn't be true. I should have listened to you and told him that night. Maybe I could have stopped her taking the boys.' She fell quiet as the bedroom door opened and Roy came in with a wary look on his face.

'Right,' Jane said, 'I'll leave you two to talk. Come down when you're ready. I'll make a start on breakfast.'

* * *

'Sam.' Roy pulled her into his arms. 'I'm sorry, sweetheart.'

'No, *I'm* sorry,' she said, sobbing against his chest. 'I should have told you, but I was so scared of what it might mean. I should have trusted you.'

He kissed the top of her head. 'I understand why you thought what you did but believe me, it'll never happen. I'm yours, forever.'

'I know.' She reached up and kissed him. 'Any news from Jack?'

He shook his head. 'I guess he'll call me after she's had the scan. I need to call Livvy's parents again, put them in the picture and see if they've a contact number for Hank. Do you feel ready to come downstairs? We'll get the boys back and then that's it, she's not having them again without supervision. I'll get my solicitor onto it right away.'

The smell of frying bacon met them as they went into the kitchen and sat down at the breakfast table. Jane poured them mugs of coffee.

'Okay, you two?'

Sammy nodded. 'We are.' She smiled at Roy, who smiled back.

'Get this down you.' Jane handed them plates laden with bacon and eggs. 'Got a feeling you're in for a heck of a day.' She handed Eddie a plate too and sat down next to him. Jess and Jon came into the kitchen. 'Help yourselves to breakfast,' she said. 'It's all in the oven, keeping warm.'

'Everything okay?' Jon asked as Jess went to fill two plates. 'Has Jack called?'

'Not yet,' Roy said. 'Erm, we've got another problem – Livvy's pissed off to LA with the kids.' He explained what had happened.

'Well, that's all you need,' Jess said, handing Jon his breakfast. 'What a devious woman, breaking into the cottage like that and then lying to you! I can hardly believe it of Livvy.'

Sammy snorted. 'I can! She didn't break in though – she must have used Harley's key. God knows how she bypassed the burglar alarm. It's Nick's birth year. How the hell did she guess that?'

'She probably took a chance and got it right first time,' Roy said. 'Ashlea Grange is Harley's birth year.'

Jane smiled. 'Ours is Jess's.'

Roy pushed his half-empty plate away and glanced at his watch. 'Thanks, Jane. I'd better call Peter and Gina again. I'll use the phone in the lounge.'

'I'll come with you,' Sammy said, jumping to her feet.

* * *

'So you had no idea she wasn't allowed to take the boys out of the country without my permission?' Roy asked. Peter had just told him he didn't have a contact number for Hank, just Livvy's cell phone.

'We had no idea at all, Roy. If we'd known, we'd have done something to stop her.'

'She actually stole the passports from our home. I'm worried she's not going to bring the boys back. Also...' Roy hesitated momentarily. He didn't want to freak Peter out, but he needed to be told – Harley was his granddaughter after all. 'Harley's back in hospital. She had a stroke last night. I really need to get in touch with Livvy and she's not answering my calls.'

'Oh, the poor wee girl,' Peter said. 'As if Harley's not had enough to deal with. I'm sorry I can't help you, Roy. Would you like us to contact Livvy and pass on the message to call you urgently?'

'Err, leave it for now,' Roy said. 'If I can't get hold of her today, I'll get back to you.' The last thing he wanted was Livvy getting prior warning he was on to her and vanishing altogether with the kids although the fact that her daughter was so ill should make her come back and face the music.

'What about getting in touch with her friend Sheena? Livvy

will have confided in her, I'm sure. She may even have given her Hank's number.'

'There's a thought. Do you have Sheena's number?'

'One minute while I ask Gina.' The line went muffled and then Peter was back: 'We think this is it, but Gina's not too sure as it's an old number.' He rattled off a mobile number and Roy scribbled it down, thanked him and said goodbye.

'Let's give this a try,' he said to Sammy. But the number was unobtainable.

'So, what now?' Sammy grabbed his hand. The phone rang out in his other hand and made her jump. 'Jack,' she said, looking at the screen.

Roy spoke to Jack while Sammy paced the room, her fingers crossed. 'Well?' she said as he hung up.

'We can go in to see her this afternoon. She's had a comfortable night, the scan's been done. I guess we'll find out more later.'

'I'll get some things together to take in. We'll call at the cottage on the way. Better for her to have her own toiletries and familiar stuff around her.'

Roy nodded. 'I'm ready for another coffee.'

'Any luck?' Jane asked as they rejoined the others in the kitchen.

Roy shook his head. 'Nope. But Harley's had a good night. Livvy's dad gave us Sheena's mobile number but it's unobtainable. I can't even recall what her surname is, otherwise we could try directory enquiries.' He stopped as Jon spluttered on his coffee.

Jess took his mug from him and thumped him on the back: 'You okay, love?'

He nodded and coughed. 'Went down the wrong way,' he gasped, eyes watering. Jane passed him a sheet of kitchen roll and he blew his nose. 'Shall we get off home?' he suggested when he'd recovered. 'Roy will call us if there's any news. We should pop in and see the babies later and Nathan will probably ring for a lift from the station.'

Jess got to her feet. 'I'll go and pack our bags.'

'I'll see to *our* bags, Ed,' Jane said. 'We should get back and maybe *we* can go and see the babies tonight.'

'Okay,' Eddie said. 'I'll nip to the little boys' room. Don't forget to bring the car keys down, Jane – they're on the bedside table.' Sammy followed Jane out of the room and Roy frowned as Jon fidgeted in his seat: 'You okay, Jon?'

'Err, yeah. Fancy a quick fag? I need a word. Outside,' he continued as Roy raised an eyebrow.

Roy nodded and followed him out on to the patio. He handed Jon a cigarette and lit one for himself. 'What is it? You look a bit bothered.'

Jon looked up at the open guest bedroom windows above and beckoned Roy around the corner. 'I've, err, I've got Sheena's current mobile number,' he whispered. 'Add it to your phone, quick.'

Roy whipped his phone from his jeans pocket and added the number Jon quoted.

'Thanks, Jon. I take it Jess doesn't know you've got this?'

'Nobody does, except Livvy. For God's sake, don't say anything to Jess. It was a one-off, a long time ago.'

'But you're still in touch with Sheena?'

'Occasionally.'

'So how do I explain to Sammy how I got it?'

'Fuck!' Jon ran his hands through his curls. 'I don't know. But you need it and that's all that matters at the moment. It's a chance I'll have to take.'

'I'll do my best to keep you out of it though Christ knows how. Sammy's bound to want an answer as to how I got it and I'm not lying to her.'

'I'll leave it with you,' Jon said. 'Ah, here's Jess.'

'What are you two up to, hiding around the corner?' she said with a grin. 'You've got guilt written all over you.'

Roy smiled and put his arm around Jess. She was his goddaughter and he loved her dearly. She'd been engaged to his late son, Nick. The thought that Jon had cheated on her with Livvy's mate made him feel sick, even though he'd no right to feel that way after what he'd done in the past. But Jon had said it was a long time ago and he believed him. 'Stops the smoke wafting into the house. You okay, Granny?' he teased, squeezing her. 'Let's hope those babies are doing alright when you visit later.'

'Yes, I hope they'll still let them home next week. We'll manage to look after them between us all. Give Harley our love and tell Jack we'll speak to him when he gets a minute to call us,' Jess said. 'Come on, you,' she said to Jon, 'let's go home.'

Roy stared after the pair as they went back indoors. They seemed happy enough, they always did, but who knew? He looked at his phone and blew out his cheeks. *You solve one problem and it presents another*, he thought, and went back inside to say his goodbyes.

* * *

'What shall we do today?' Hank asked as he and Livvy lay in bed, basking in the afterglow of early-morning lovemaking and savouring the last few minutes before the boys got up. It was the last day he'd wake with her in his arms for a while and he hated the thought.

'Let's have a lazy day around the pool,' she said. 'Looks like it's going to be another scorcher. Too warm to drag the kids around, they'll only get tetchy.'

'Fine by me. They're sleeping in late. They were awake in the middle of the night, messing about with your phone. God knows who they'd dialled, if anyone, but it was all lit up. I just switched it off before they ran up a huge bill. Little monkeys! Shall we have breakfast in peace?'

Livvy smiled and slid out of bed. She grabbed a T-shirt and knickers from a drawer and pulled them on. 'I'll go and fix the coffee and you can make the pancakes,' she said, laughing as he gazed at her with a silly smile on his face. 'I know,' she said as he opened his mouth to speak, 'I've got one sexy ass!' She imitated his drawl and ran out of the room.

'I'll take a shower first,' he called as she hurried to the kitchen and put the coffee maker on. Her phone lay on the counter beside the sink. She switched it on and frowned as it beeped with messages and missed calls, all from Roy. She checked the times: the last call was half an hour ago. She froze as she realised one was in the early hours of the morning, LA time. Shit! If the boys had the phone at that time maybe they'd answered it. They certainly wouldn't have known what they were doing, but RJ often walked around with the TV remote, pressing buttons and pretending he was talking on a phone. They both had toy mobiles that played tunes and sang messages. She looked at a couple of texts asking her to call Roy ASAP. What the hell was so urgent that it couldn't wait until tomorrow when she'd be back on UK soil?

RJ ran into the kitchen and wrapped himself around her legs, followed by Danny, who did likewise. She gave them both a hug. 'Sit down, boys.' She handed out bowls of Cheerios and orange juice and sat down with them. She could hear Hank singing, so he was still in the shower. 'Boys, did you play with Mommy's phone last night?'

Danny nodded solemnly, while RJ screwed up his nose and laughed. 'Daddy talked,' he said.

'Did he?' Livvy felt her stomach lurch.

Danny smiled. 'On the phone,' he said, pointing. 'Daddy say, "Hello boys."'

'Shit!' Livvy muttered, switching off the phone as it rang

out. She pushed it into her handbag on the worktop as Hank came into the kitchen.

'You okay, honey?' he asked, dropping a kiss on top of her head. 'Right, who wants pancakes?' he said laughing as RJ and Danny shouted 'Me!'

'Baby?' he directed at Livvy.

'Just a couple for me,' she said, smiling. She wasn't going to let Roy spoil their last day together, not if she could help it. She really didn't want to go home to that mausoleum of a house. She'd loved Ashlea Grange when Roy had bought it – her dream home. But the place quickly lost its appeal when he left her. Even though Harley and Jack had lived with her, she'd been lonely when they'd been out with friends and the boys were in bed. Going back to that life held no charms for her. Hank's large ranch was homely, chaotic and friendly, with his family dropping in constantly – she knew she could be happy and settled there.

'Been thinking, hon,' Hank began, deftly flipping pancakes over on the griddle pan. 'Why don't we change our flights? You can extend your trip a few days and I'll get us all on the same flight home? Call Roy and ask him if he minds you staying the rest of the week with me. I don't want to let you go, I feel like I've found the girl I married again. Then also, you wouldn't have to struggle back alone with the boys.'

Livvy chewed her lip. Dare she say yes? She was very tempted. Roy would go mental. What if he decided to drive up to Glasgow to look for her? But why should he? What if she called him, told him her mum wasn't well and her dad's back was playing up and he couldn't take care of her? Would he buy it? It was worth a try. Hank was looking at her with such a loving expression, she owed it to him to try.

She nodded. 'I'll call him later.'

'Let's take breakfast onto the deck then,' Hank said with a big smile on his face.

15

Jon walked into the Special Care Baby unit and found Jess cuddling Molly. He'd dropped her off earlier and gone on to pick their son Nathan up from the station.

He'd taken him back to their family home and then spent half an hour driving around to clear his head, going over the earlier conversation he'd had with Roy. He felt there'd been no choice other than to pass on Sheena's number even though it might land him well and truly in the shit. His head was thumping and it felt stifling in the unit. He stood watching Jess; she looked bursting with happiness. She caught him staring and her stunning blue eyes lit up with a smile.

'You're going to be a fabulous grandma,' he said. 'They'll be spoilt rotten.' She was in her element, had always wanted another baby, but he'd been unable to oblige due to a vasectomy shortly after the births of Jack and Nathan.

'I'm so thrilled,' she said, 'I can't tell you how much. Anyway, you'll be a smashing granddad. Can't wait to get them home. Maybe they and Jack could move in with us for a while until Harley's discharged, or I could move into the cottage with him to help? He won't be able to manage on his own.'

Jon nodded. 'Let's not jump the gun just yet. Jack and Harley need to make their own decisions about what to do for the best. And I think you should give Jack a bit more credit than that – he's a dab hand with them.'

'Well, so were you with ours but there were two of us.'

'Yes, and ours were a bit bigger.' He put on a plastic apron, washed his hands, sat down beside her and took hold of Molly while Jess got Ben out of his incubator.

Jon tickled Molly beneath her chin and she reached up and held on to his finger, her tiny hand grasping tightly. His heart gave a little lurch as he thought back to when the boys were newborn and how happy he and Jess had been. He'd always loved her from the minute he'd clapped eyes on her when he was four years old. They'd been brought up as brother and sister by his dad Eddie and Jess's mum, his step-mum, Jane. He'd been in his early twenties when he found out that Eddie wasn't his biological father. By which time he and Jess had fallen in love and thought they were in an incestuous relationship. Thank goodness they weren't, he thought now, as Jess was already pregnant with their sons. He'd been devoted to her until the day he met Livvy's friend Sheena and had a one-night stand with her. He wished with all his heart he could turn back the clock and he'd tried hard to put it behind him. He'd lost contact with Sheena and even deleted her mobile number from his phone but she'd sent him a new number a few months ago and for some reason he hadn't bothered to get rid of it. Perhaps as well now with Roy's kids going missing, but still, he wished she hadn't sent it. It would destroy Jess if news of his fling ever got out. He couldn't bear to lose her, she was everything to him.

'You okay, Jon?' Jess's voice broke his thoughts. 'You're miles away. Molly's looking directly at you. Aw, bless her, little darling. Oh, God, I just hope Harley makes a good recovery – these babies need her.'

Jon took her hand as her eyes filled. He choked back his

own tears. They were all so emotional at the moment. 'She'll be fine, Jess. Roy said it will take time, but we all know what Harley's like. She beat the odds with leukaemia. There's no holding that girl down.'

She nodded. 'I haven't even asked you how Nathan is. Bet he's brought me back a ton of dirty laundry.'

''Fraid so, a bloody big holdall full! He's fine, didn't get the job with the band. Well actually, that's not strictly correct. He *did* get the job but turned it down. Played a few gigs but said the other band members weren't very professional in their attitude, so he's dumped them rather than the other way round. He said he might ask Dad if there's any chance of him playing on the next Raiders' tour as an extra.'

'Really?' Jess raised an eyebrow. 'That would give him a good grounding if they'll have him on board. Are they not too old for him though?'

'Heck no! Zak Starkey, Ringo's lad, plays drums with The Who. He fits in great. Well, you've seen him. He was on the *Quadrophenia* tour, remember?'

'I do. He was very good. I recall you telling me that Moonie had taught him when he was a little lad. Just like Roy taught Nathan to play guitar. Well, if Nathan gets a chance like that, it could be the making of him and at least we'll know where he is and who he's with! Can't get up to too much mischief on the grumpy old man tour!'

Jon laughed. 'Better not say that in front of Dad and Roy but peace of mind will be a novelty. We haven't had much of that with Nathan, have we?' He looked up as Sammy came into the room. 'Hi, Sam, come to play granny with Jess?' He waited while she fastened a plastic apron around her waist and washed her hands and then handed Molly to her. 'I'll leave you girls alone and pop out for a fag, then nip up and see Harley.'

'Roy's outside, too,' Sammy said. 'Jack's in with Harley.'

'Okay, see you later.' Jon hurried away and met up with Roy in the car park.

'How are the twins?' Roy asked and handed Jon a cigarette.

'Seem to be doing great,' Jon said. 'Err, any luck with Sheena?'

'Not yet. Message service was on. I didn't leave her one obviously. I'll try her again when we get back home.'

'You didn't say anything to Sam?'

'What do you take me for, Jon?' Roy took a long drag on his cigarette and puffed a cloud of smoke above his head. 'Told you I'll do my best to keep your name out of it.'

'Thanks. How's Harley?'

Roy shrugged. 'Holding her own. They're doing more tests to find out the extent of the damage. She's still slurring her words and her left arm and leg are limp. Once she gets the feeling back, they'll start her on physiotherapy, they said.'

'A long job then?'

'Seems that way. She was asking for her mother earlier. I've gotta get hold of Livvy today, no matter what – she needs to get her arse back here with my kids.'

'What'll happen when she *does* come back? Will the boys be taken off her?'

'I spoke to my solicitor before we came here. An out-of-office-hours call that will cost me the earth, no doubt. He said he'd get a care order sorted and they'll come to me and Sam. Livvy will only be allowed to see them under supervision. Basically she's fucked up big style for taking them away.'

'But Danny isn't yours. Doesn't that count?'

'Not sure how that'll work long term. I may lose him to her eventually but I'll bloody fight her for him! She's not fit to look after two kids on her own.'

'She's got Hank though,' Jon pointed out. 'He seems a decent guy, a family man.'

'Yes, he does. And I have a feeling he doesn't know she

nicked the passports. Well, he soon will. Let him sort her out –
I've had my fill of her to last a lifetime.' He threw his butt end
down and ground it out with the heel of his boot. 'I'd better go
back inside. Are you coming up to see Harley in a bit?'

Jon nodded. 'I'll follow you in.'

Jack looked up as the door opened and Roy came back into the
room. He felt glad to see him. He'd been trying to get Harley to
take a sip of tea from a lidded beaker but she kept pushing it
away. He couldn't understand what she was trying to say to him
and he blinked away tears of frustration. 'See if she'll have a
drink from you, Roy.' He handed the cup over and Roy sat
down.

'Are you being awkward, princess?' Roy said to Harley. He
winked at her and held the beaker to her lips. She took a couple
of sips and then shook her head. 'Think she's had enough. Take
yourself off to the café and get a bite to eat, Jack. Your dad's
coming up shortly. Go and see your babies, do you good to take
a break.'

'Thanks. Are you sure you don't mind?'

'Course not, go on. We'll be fine, won't we, princess?'

Harley nodded and waved her right hand at Jack. He bent
to kiss her and left the room.

He found his mum and Sammy with the twins and they
smiled at him.

'Oh, Jack,' his mum Jess said and her eyes filled with tears.
'You look weary, darling. Have you eaten today?'

'I had breakfast earlier. How are they doing?'

'Good, we've fed them,' she said. 'Both are sleeping now so
we're about to put them down and go for a coffee. Why don't
you join us and grab a sandwich? We've a few things we'd like to
discuss with you.'

'Okay. Sounds good to me.'

* * *

Sammy carried a laden tray across to Jess and Jack, who were seated by the café window overlooking the Maternity Department car park. 'Here you go, get stuck in. Has your mum run the plan by you?'

Jack nodded, tearing the wrappings from a pack of ham salad sandwiches.

'What do you think?' Sammy asked. She and Jess had discussed caring for the twins between them with the help of Jane while Jack finished his last year at uni.

'It's a good idea, in principle, but I think I'd rather be at Mum's than the cottage, at least until Harley's allowed home.'

Jess smiled. 'That's fine. We can all muck in, no matter where you are. We'll get the men to bring the cots and stuff over this week and I'll see if I can find a painter to freshen up your old room.'

'I'll call you later with the number of the guy we use,' Sammy said. 'I'm sure he'll squeeze you in if you tell him it's an emergency.'

'I don't even know yet if they'll be home this week,' Jack said. 'But I guess we should be prepared just in case. They said today they're going to start Harley on physiotherapy. There's someone coming to see her tomorrow to assess her. I offered to take her down to see the twins earlier but she didn't want to go.'

'She will when she's feeling up to it,' Jess said, patting his hand. 'Has Roy had any luck getting hold of Livvy yet?'

Jack shook his head. 'Not while I've been with him.'

Sammy took a sip of coffee and stared out of the window, deep in thought. If it wasn't for the kids, she wouldn't care if Livvy never came back. But Harley was asking for her and Roy needed his boys' home. She'd told Jess what had happened while they were feeding the babies.

Jess sighed. 'She's blown it now. Roy won't let them out of his sight when she returns. God, Sam, we're really going to have our hands full, aren't we? Kids coming out of our ears.'

Sammy raised an eyebrow. 'Just a bit!'

* * *

Roy paced the floor of the music room, waiting for his call to be answered. This was the third time he'd tried Sheena's number today and at last it was ringing. A breathless voice said, 'Hello, hang on, I'm driving!' Then, 'Sorry about that. Had to pull over.'

'Sheena? This is Roy Cantello,' he began. 'Sorry to bother you, but I need to get hold of Livvy. She's not answering my calls. I'm led to believe she's in LA with Hank and I wondered if you have a contact number for their home?'

He heard a sharp intake of breath and then she was gabbling that no, she didn't have a number except for Livvy's and should she call her?

Roy stared up at the ceiling, silent for a moment. Livvy might run scared if Sheena called her. How much did Sheena know? Had Livvy confided in her about stealing the passports? The only way to make sure she didn't run further was to tell Livvy about Harley. But was it fair to put that responsibility on Sheena's shoulders? 'Err, thanks. I really do need her to contact me urgently. Harley's been taken ill, she's asking for Livvy.'

'Sorry to hear that, Roy. Is it serious?'

'Yes, she's had a stroke. Complications from her pregnancy.'

There was silence, then, 'Jesus! I'm so sorry.' The line went dead and Roy thought he must have lost connection. He tried again but got the messaging service.

* * *

Sheena sat in the lay-by, stunned by Roy's news. Harley was the same age as her own lively young daughter, Cassie. What a dreadful thing to happen. She felt sorry for Roy, who obviously now knew Livvy was away with his boys when she shouldn't be. She wondered how he'd got her number. Must have been from Jon, she thought. What the hell should she do? She *did* have Hank's house number but it wasn't up to her to pass on that sort of news. She felt angry with Livvy. If she'd wanted to spend time with Hank, she should have gone on her own and left the boys with Roy. He'd sounded worried to death. He had enough to cope with and although he didn't say so, must be frantic about their whereabouts. She looked up the number in her contacts, scribbled it down and called Roy back. The action might lose her Livvy's friendship, but it was a chance she was willing to take.

* * *

Sammy picked up Roy's ringing phone from the kitchen table. She didn't recognise the number, but answered anyway. The caller, a female with a Scottish accent, asked to speak to Roy, who was outside. Sammy frowned. It wasn't Livvy; *her* accent wasn't so strong these days.

'One minute, I'll give him a shout. May I ask who's calling? Oh, right, hang on, he's here now.' She handed the phone to him, mouthing, 'It's Sheena.'

'Roy Cantello,' he said, raising an eyebrow at Sammy, who was looking intently at him. 'You do. Okay, yes, yes, I understand your position. Thank you. Get me a pen,' he said to Sammy. She handed him one and he scribbled down a number in the margin of a newspaper on the table. 'I really do appreciate this, Sheena. Yes, I'm sure she will. But you do know she shouldn't have taken the boys out of the country without my consent, don't you? She actually told you that? You won't? Okay, thanks again. Yes, I'll call you when I get hold of her.'

Sammy was looking at him quizzically as he ended the call.

'So how did she get your number?'

'I called her earlier. The number will have been stored in her phone.'

'But I thought the number you had for her was unobtainable.'

He took a deep breath. 'It was – I was given a different one.'

'By whom?'

'Jesus, Sam, is there any need for this inquisition?'

'No. I'm just curious how you got her number, that's all.' She sat down and stared at him.

'Does it really matter? I need to call Hank.'

'I know you do, but yes, it matters. No more secrets, remember?'

'Jon, I got it from Jon.'

'Jon!' She frowned. 'Harley told me she thought he had a thing for Sheena. They were very friendly. So he's still in touch?'

'Apparently not. But she sent him her new number a while ago. Perhaps as well she did, given today's circumstances. Look, don't say anything to Jess. There's nothing going on – it was over before it began, according to Jon. No point in upsetting anybody.'

'I wouldn't dream of it. There's no way I'd put Jess through what I went through. What else did Sheena say?'

'She knew about the passports and the LA trip but had been sworn to secrecy. I guess I rattled her conscience when I told her about Harley. Right, I need to get my head into gear now and call Hank's place.'

* * *

Hank took a deep breath and sank down onto a kitchen chair. He lit a cigarette, his hand shaking. Livvy had taken the boys to the drugstore for candy and he'd just spoken to Roy Cantello. He drew deeply on his cigarette, feeling shocked and slightly sickened by what Roy had told him. Sickened, because he knew Livvy would be devastated when he broke the news of Harley's stroke, but also, he couldn't believe her deceit at stealing the boys' passports. Not only that, she'd lied quite openly when she'd told him Roy had given his permission for her to bring the boys here. He couldn't begin to imagine what Roy was going through at the moment. His heart had gone out to the guy. Harley was a lovely kid and similar in age to his youngest girl. He brushed away sudden tears. He'd made Roy a promise that he would bring his sons home as soon as he could arrange flights and he'd assured him that he would travel with them.

He looked up as the door opened and RJ and Danny ran in, clutching paper bags, followed by Livvy. She smiled and put her arms around his shoulders and dropped a kiss on the top of his head. He pushed her away and got to his feet, shooing the boys out onto the deck.

She frowned and took a step backwards. 'Honey, why did you push me away?'

He stared at her. 'I just spoke to Roy Cantello,' he said and watched the colour drain from her face. 'Your daughter Harley is seriously ill. Seems like Roy's been trying to contact you but you've been ignoring his calls and texts. Now why would that be, Livvy?'

16

Livvy ignored Hank's question and grabbed him by the arm. 'What's wrong with Harley? Is it serious? Are the babies okay?' She felt the room spinning and Hank caught her as she dropped to the floor.

He patted her cheeks and brought her a glass of water. 'Sorry to shock you like that, but it's no more of a shock than the one I got from your ex. You've totally screwed that guy up, he wants his kids back.'

Livvy took a sip of water. She sat back against the wall and took a deep breath. 'And he'll get them, when I take them home. But never mind him, what's wrong with my Harley?'

Hank explained and she shook her head. 'My poor little girl, as if she hasn't had enough. Oh God!' She ran her hands through her curls. 'I need to be with her. What do I do now? Roy will kill me when I get back.'

'I doubt it. But he's pretty mad. You get right on the phone and you apologise big-time for what you've done. How the fuck did you get into his house for the passports? Did you break in?'

'I err, I... had a key cut from Harley's,' she stammered. 'I waited until I knew the house was empty.'

She felt sick as Hank glared at her. She'd never seen him look so angry.

'I thought I knew you,' he said and walked out of the room.

Livvy waited a minute or two and then followed him. She found him throwing the boys' clothes into a suitcase. Their passports lay on the bed and he grabbed hold of them as she reached to pick them up. 'No you don't,' he muttered.

'What are you doing?'

'Getting ready to take the boys home. I'm gonna call the airline in a minute and book flights for tonight if possible. Those kids are going straight back to their father and *I'm* taking them.'

'You can't do that, you're not giving my boys to Roy.'

'Livvy, you lost your rights to those kids the moment you took them out of the UK without his permission. I can't believe you did that. What if he'd done it to you? How would you feel? And to top it all, he's got a very sick daughter on his hands and two new-born grandchildren who need their mom. Are you so selfish that you can only think about what *you* want?'

'That's not fair,' she yelled. 'I did it for you, so that we could be together.'

'Don't you dare put the blame on me! I thought you'd got Roy's permission. No way did I tell you to steal the damn passports.' He shook his head. 'You should have told me the truth, stayed home even. I would have been back in a couple more days. You could have just visited your folks and then gone home. Now your parents will think badly of *me*, and that maybe I had something to do with this.'

'I'm sorry.'

'It's Roy you should be apologising to. Do it now.'

'I can't. He already thinks badly of me.' She burst into tears but he didn't come to her, just carried on packing, ignoring her. He hated her, she just knew it. This was all Roy's fault. He'd ruined things with his stupid rules. The boys were fine with her. It's not as if she didn't look after them. She watched as Hank locked the case and pushed her out of the way as he stood it by the door. She grabbed her handbag from the bed and ran out of the room.

* * *

Hank stared after her and then moved to the window as the engine of the Jeep turned over. He watched as the wheels spun and she sped off down the drive, dust and gravel flying in all directions. Shit, she'd never driven it before. It was a big vehicle for such a little lady. RJ and Danny appeared in the doorway, complaining they were hungry.

'Want Mommy,' RJ said, pouting.

'Mommy won't be long, boys. Let's find you some lunch then we're going on a big adventure, just the three of us.' He got down on his knees and cuddled them close. Poor little guys, they needed stability, and much as it pained him to admit it, he didn't think Livvy was the one to give it. 'Hank's gonna take you home to see Daddy and Sammy.'

Danny's face lit up. 'See Daddy? Yes!' he cried and RJ jumped up and down. 'Going on big plane, RJ,' Danny said, nodding excitedly.

Hank made sandwiches and gave them drinks of juice. He sat them at the kitchen table and went back into the bedroom to pack a case for himself. He tried Livvy's cell phone but she wasn't picking up. He wondered what the hell he should do. He called the airline, changed his flight and managed to get seats for the boys. They would be leaving later today. Livvy would have to take a chance to get a flight and if not... well, she had her return ticket for tomorrow. He called Roy and told him of his plans and that he would bring the boys directly to Jasmine House. Roy sounded relieved, thanked him profusely and offered to pick them up from the airport.

Back in the kitchen, Hank poured coffee and sat down with

the boys. He tried Livvy's phone again and left her a message. If she chose to ignore it then there was nothing he could do. He'd take those kids back even if it destroyed his marriage. The way he felt about her at the moment wasn't a good feeling. He loved her but needed a woman he could trust, one that would trust *him* enough to confide in him.

* * *

Livvy pulled up at a gas station. She hadn't a clue where she was. She'd driven blindly, not checking road signs, until she'd noticed she was almost out of fuel. Cursing, she struggled with the fuel cap and filled the Jeep. She knew she should call Hank – he'd be worrying and her boys would be missing her. She paid for the gas and a bottle of ice-cold water.

She checked her phone: it showed missed calls from Hank. She started up the engine and drove a few miles further along the straight and dusty road and pulled into a parking bay. She took a long drink of water, wondering how Roy had managed to get hold of Hank's number. There was only one person in the UK she'd given it to, one person she could trust. Sheena wouldn't betray her confidence even in an emergency, would she?

Hank didn't sound particularly friendly when he picked up. 'Where the hell are you?'

'I've no idea.'

'Well, you need to get your ass back here. The boys are crying.'

She could hear RJ and Danny jabbering in the background; they didn't sound unhappy. She sighed.

'We need to talk. I'm leaving in a couple of hours for the airport.'

'The airport?'

'I booked flights for tonight. I'm taking the boys home.'

'Not without me, you're not,' she yelled. 'Those are my kids.'

'Well, when you get back, you can get on to the airline and try and book a flight with us. Otherwise you'll have to go home tomorrow, as planned.'

'But I'm flying back to Glasgow. I need to pick up my car from my parents' place.'

'Not my problem.'

She stared at the phone as he hung up. Why was he taking Roy's side in this? Couldn't he see that if they kept the boys in the US, they could fight for custody over here? But then there was Harley and the babies. She needed to see them. What a mess. She started up the Jeep, did a U-turn and headed back in the direction she came from.

* * *

Roy waited with Sammy in arrivals, checking the board constantly. He breathed a sigh of relief when he saw the flight Hank and the boys were on had landed.

'Thank God for that,' he said.

Sammy grasped his hand. 'Do you think she'll be with him?'

'I hope not – I don't want a scene in front of the kids.'

They waited for what seemed like ages and then Hank appeared with a luggage trolley, RJ balanced on top of the bags, and Danny trotting along by his side. Hank looked weary. Roy felt sorry for him. Travelling with two little kids on your own at his age was no picnic.

Danny spotted them first and shrieked, 'Daddy!' He ran forwards and dodged below the barrier. Roy picked him up and hugged him tight, his eyes filling.

Hank helped RJ down off the trolley and he ran towards them, giggling, his thick black fringe flopping up and down. Roy handed Danny to Sammy and scooped RJ up, cuddling him close.

Roy turned to Hank, who stood nearby looking awkward. There was no sign of Livvy.

'Mate, I can't tell you how much I appreciate this,' Roy said, his voice husky with tears. 'I thought I'd never see them again. Come on, let's get you home.'

Hank followed with the bags and they all squeezed into Roy's BMW, the boys both talking at once. Sammy sat between their car seats in the back. Danny told her all about the big plane and the dark sky and RJ nodded his approval.

'Don't suppose they slept much?' Roy said to Hank.

'Actually they did,' he replied. 'Pretty soon into the flight. They were real good boys. They've been awake a couple of hours, but they'll be a bit out of timing for a day or two. Err, do you have a key to Ashlea Grange? I never thought to get one from Livvy.'

'I do,' Roy said. 'But look, you can stay with us tonight if you like. What's your plan? And what about Livvy?'

'She couldn't get a seat on the flight. She's flying back later today to Glasgow to pick up her car. Thanks for the offer but I'll stay at The Grange until she gets back. Then, depending on what happens, I may go back to LA. I expect she'll want to stick around to be near your daughter. How *is* Harley, by the way?'

'Not so great,' Roy replied. 'It's going to be a long job getting her back on her feet. Livvy should really be here for her.'

Hank shook his head. 'I can't imagine what you're going through. If it were one of mine...'

'Well, at least I've got my boys home. That's one worry out of the way. Now I can concentrate on seeing that Harley gets the best help available.'

'The babies are definitely being allowed home on Wednesday,' Sammy chipped in. 'We were told last night.'

'That's great news,' Hank said. 'You're going to have your hands full.'

'We've got a rota worked out,' Sammy said. 'There are enough of us. They're going to Jack's parents' place to start with and we'll all be on hand to help.'

Roy pulled up outside Jasmine House. 'At least come in and have breakfast with us, Hank, then you can see the boys settling in. No doubt Livvy will want a report when you next speak to her.'

'Thanks, Roy. I will, if you don't mind.'

Sammy joined Roy and Hank at the kitchen table. Roy pushed the coffee pot towards her. She helped herself and sat back, smiling. The boys were in their playroom, making a racket – they'd already argued over the Lego. She'd leave them to play for a while, give them an early lunch and then put them down for a nap while Roy went to see Harley. Sammy had called Jane to let her know the boys were home and Jane had promised to come over later to keep her company. She was planning to make the most of today before Livvy got back. God knows how she'd fit into the scheme of things with the baby rota, but as an official grandma, she had more rights than Sammy's step-gran status.

Ah well, she wasn't going to let those thoughts spoil the first day of their new lives with the boys. There'd still be the court case in a few months, but from what Roy's solicitor had told them, they stood a really good chance of winning sole custody. And if Livvy wanted to stay married to Hank, she'd have to move to LA and just have scheduled visits here with RJ and Danny. It sounded simple enough, but Sammy had a gut feeling that Livvy wouldn't give up easily, not on her boys, nor her claims on Roy.

17

Livvy spotted her parents who were waiting for her in the arrivals hall. She took a deep breath and put on a smile. Her dad looked angry and her mum's red eyes seemed like she had shed more than a few tears.

Her dad gave her a curt nod. 'How was your flight?'

'Umm, okay,' she muttered and looked at her mum for support. Her dad took the handle of her suitcase and set off in front of them at a quick pace, dragging the case behind him.

'He's mad at me, isn't he?' She linked her arm through her mum's. Her dad had never uttered a cross word to her since their reunion. Him being furious with her wasn't a feeling she liked.

'Not so much at what you did, but more because you didn't trust us enough to tell us what was going on,' her mum said. 'It was very wrong to take the boys away like that. You should have left them with us if you wanted to spend some time with Hank. So, I assume they're now back home with Roy? Your call kept breaking up yesterday so I couldn't quite make out what you were saying.'

'Everybody hates me. Hank turned against me too,' Livvy

sobbed, unable to stop the tears tumbling. 'He took the boys home to Roy yesterday. Hank's waiting for me at Ashlea Grange. I think he's going to tell me that our marriage is over, Mom. He said he doesn't trust me any more.'

'Oh, hen, try not to think like that. Maybe you just need to talk. But the one thing you have to do is stay in the UK. Harley is going to need all the help you can give her *and* the babies. Your marriage will survive if Hank's the right one for you. Anyway,' she continued as they reached the car park, 'we're coming back with you to Cheshire for a couple of weeks so we can lend a hand with the babies and everything. Maybe Roy will let you have the boys for the odd day if we're around.'

Livvy flung her arms around her mum. 'I doubt it, but thank you so much. I was dreading going home with no one in my corner – I almost feel like running away. I think even Sheena has betrayed my confidence.'

Her dad turned and shook his head. 'No, you're wrong there. Sheena hasn't betrayed you. She did what she thought was right. You did yourself no favours in refusing to take Roy's calls. That poor man was beside himself. You've betrayed yourself, so stop whingeing and get a grip. You can't keep using the wee fellas as pawns. They need stability and right now *we* don't think you're the one to give it. And believe me, I'm not saying this lightly. No one knows more than me and your mother how painful giving up a child is. Now get in the car and you can go and make your peace with Sheena later.'

Livvy got in the car and stared out of the window, feeling totally bereft. Maybe her dad and Hank were right. Maybe she *was* being selfish, thinking only of herself and using the boys to get at Roy. She felt lost without them. Surely once the case went to court she'd be sure to get custody of Danny, if not RJ? She'd certainly fight her corner where Danny was concerned. If the court took into account he wasn't even Roy's flesh and blood, it had to go in her favour.

* * *

'So why didn't you call *me* first to tell me about Harley before you called Roy back?' Livvy demanded after listening to Sheena's account of what happened and why she had taken the action she did.

Sheena was sitting opposite her in the lounge of her Dennistoun home. Her body language spoke volumes. She was distant and unsmiling. 'I did what I felt I had to do,' she said, sitting with her arms folded across her middle. 'It wasn't my responsibility to tell you about Harley. Roy was in bits. I called him back as soon as I regained composure. Under the circumstances I couldn't lie to him. I told you before you went that I didn't approve of what you were up to – I don't know how you can even think you've been wronged.'

'Well, thanks to you, I've lost my boys. Roy's got them back.'

Sheena jumped to her feet and paced the floor. 'Would you just listen to yourself? It's time you took responsibility for your own actions. Jon's had to put his marriage on the line to give Roy my number. Good job Jess doesn't know that or he'd be in deep shit and none of this is his fault. I'm not apologising, Livvy. Like I said, I did what I felt I had to do.'

Livvy chewed her lip. She'd never argued with Sheena before but even listening to her side of things, she still felt wronged. Her friend should at least have warned her that Roy knew of her whereabouts. No doubt the outcome would have been the same, but she might have been prepared and taken Roy's next call rather than have him speak to Hank.

She picked up her handbag from the floor and stood up. 'I'd better go, I've a long day tomorrow. At least my parents haven't abandoned me totally. They're coming home with me for a couple of weeks while I get things sorted.' She moved towards the door, then turned back to face Sheena. A sudden thought had popped into her head: 'So you've spoken to Jon recently then?'

Sheena nodded, her cheeks flushing slightly. 'Briefly. He called to let me know he'd passed on my number, but that was after Roy spoke to me. Believe me, I had no prior warning when Roy put me on the spot.'

Livvy shrugged. 'Whatever. Well, goodnight then.'

Sheena gave her a quick hug. 'Safe journey tomorrow. Let me know how Harley is when you've seen her. There's no need for us to fall out over this, Liv. When you've had the time to think about it, you'll know you'd have done exactly the same.'

* * *

Sammy crept out of the nursery and closed the door. She leant against it, sighing with relief. Both boys were flat out at last. It had taken mugs of hot chocolate, umpteen stories and lots of cuddles and hair-stroking. Hopefully their body clocks would adjust in the next few days. She ran downstairs and poured herself a G&T. She took her drink through to the lounge, kicked off her shoes and settled on the sofa. Roy would be back soon. He'd gone to a band meeting at Phil Jackson's place. The Raiders were planning their next UK tour. Hopefully it wouldn't take him away for too many nights. Jane had promised to help if she needed it, but Jess would want help, too – they'd all be run ragged before the end of the summer.

Sammy picked up the DVD control and pressed play. The TV sprang to life. She jumped up to take out a *Fireman Sam* DVD, replaced it with The Traveling Wilburys and settled back down again. She was lost in memories and the dulcet tones of Roy Orbison when her own Roy came in. He poured himself a single malt and joined her on the sofa. She snuggled close and he put an arm around her, dropping a kiss on her lips.

'You were miles away then,' he teased. 'You okay, darling?'

'I'm fine. I was thinking about that tour you did in the sixties with Roy Orbison. Do you remember? When me, Jane and Pat came backstage and met him? I wonder what happened to the photo.'

'Jane's got it. It's in a frame on the wall in Ed's music room – you'll have to get a copy from her.' He pointed his glass at the ceiling. 'How have they been?'

'Lively,' she said with a sigh. 'Thought their bath would relax them but they were more hyper than ever. Anyway, they're zonked now. I'm just making the most of the peace. How did your meeting go?'

'Great. Nathan came along with Ed. He wants to join us on tour. It actually works out well because Phil, believe it or not, has to have a new knee. He's been limping for a while but put off seeing the doc. All that bloody jumping about on stage he's done in the past, the sliding up and down on his knees, has knackered it. Anyway, we're gonna book some studio time and if things work out, Phil can get his op done privately in the next week or so. Nathan can take his place on the tour while he recovers.'

'What about the new album? Will Phil be fit for recording?'

Roy nodded. 'He'll cope with that okay – he can sit down. Frank came to the meeting tonight and he wants us in the studio next month. It's going to be a bit tough on you, managing the kids on your own while I'm in London.'

'I'll be fine, they'll be in nursery two days a week. Maybe I'll ask for an extra day. Don't worry, you need to get this new album released before we run out of money. We've spent a fortune recently with you buying this place and you haven't really earned anything for over a year.'

'I've had the songwriting royalties, but I know what you mean. As soon as Livvy moves out of Ashlea Grange, I'll put it on the market. That'll free up well over a million. We'll survive, love.' He smiled, eyes twinkling. 'You finished your drink?'

She drained her glass and put it down on the coffee table. 'I have now.'

'Would you like another? Or would you prefer to come to bed with me and chill while we've got the chance?'

She nodded. 'Let's make the most of it. From tomorrow, life will be even more hectic.'

* * *

Livvy lay stiffly beside Hank, who had his back to her. His earlier greeting had been lukewarm but he'd prepared an evening meal for them all and made her parents feel welcome.

Her dad, maybe sensing that she and Hank needed to talk, had suggested an early night and he and her mother had made themselves scarce after dinner. The subsequent conversation between her and Hank had been stilted. He'd told her he was returning to LA on Saturday, that he needed to think seriously about whether their marriage had a future.

She told him she was staying in the UK until she was sure that her boys, and Harley and the babies, were being well looked after. He told her the twins were home and staying with Jack's parents, then sarcastically followed that with 'what did she think *she* could do that wasn't being done already?'. She ignored him and spoke to Jess to see if it was convenient to bring her parents to see the twins tomorrow. Jess asked her to leave it until Friday as things were a bit hectic, but hopefully would settle down in a day or so.

She'd come up to bed. Hank joined her, stinking of cigarettes and whisky, and fell asleep within minutes. She felt a little miffed that Jess wanted her to wait to visit. After all, they were *her* grandchildren and she had more rights than Sammy, who would no doubt be at Jess's all the time, sticking her nose in. She wondered how her boys were. She hadn't dared to call Roy, even though she'd been desperate to do so. Hank said he'd spoken to Roy this morning and the boys were fine and happy, settling back into their nursery routine. That made her feel angry too. Were they even missing her? It irked her that Roy and Hank were getting pally. Who knew what they might be thinking and saying about her?

Livvy planned to visit Harley tomorrow and was dreading bumping into Roy. She was still smarting from Sheena's betrayal and knew it was something *she* wouldn't have done, no matter what. She didn't feel she could ever trust her again. She sighed and slid out of bed. No chance of sleeping with Hank snoring heavily now. Downstairs, she poured a large vodka and took it through to the lounge. It was going to be a long, sleepless night of feeling sorry for herself. She took a big swig and sat down on the sofa.

Might as well get drunk and blot it all out.

* * *

Jack closed his eyes and let his thoughts drift. He was slumped in a chair and Harley was sleeping on the bed. She slept a lot at the moment. His mum said she needed all the rest she could get to heal. He didn't fully understand quite what had happened other than the problems during her late pregnancy were to blame. Well, no matter what, they were having no more children. He couldn't bear to lose her. He knew he was lucky she was still here. They'd grown up together and he'd loved her all his life, like his dad loved his mum, or so he told everyone.

The one thing bothering him was that Harley refused to see their babies. The doctor had given her something to dry up her milk as the drugs she was taking could affect it. Since then she'd distanced herself from the twins. Everyone told him she'd rally round in her own time. He hoped so. Life was difficult enough. His mum, gran and Sammy were doing well looking after the babies and he was so grateful for their support. They insisted he try and concentrate on his studies for his finals and spend his spare time with Harley, but he was concerned he'd lose the bond he shared with his children.

He looked up as the door opened, expecting it to be Roy, who'd texted to say he was on his way. He was shocked to see Livvy slide in and close the door.

'Jack.' She held out her arms.

He allowed a quick hug and got her a chair to sit on beside the bed. She looked as though she'd been crying: her eyes were bloodshot and she was pale.

'How is she? I can't believe this has happened.'

'Nor I. She's doing okay, slow but sure.'

'And the babies? Are you seeing much of them?'

'As much as I can. I'm staying at Mum and Dad's. She's doing a great job and she's got plenty of help.'

'Well, if there's anything I can do to help, maybe have them stay over for a night, please let me know.'

He nodded, knowing that wasn't even an option. His mother would go mad at the very suggestion. The saga of RJ and Danny going missing was enough to put him off trusting Livvy with his precious babies – ever.

She turned to the bed and took Harley's hand.

After a few minutes sitting in silence, Jack excused himself and left the room to use the loo. His heart thudded as he bumped into Roy in the corridor. Shit!

'Okay, Jack?' Roy asked, giving him a pat on the back.

'Err, yeah, sort of.' Jack raised an eyebrow. 'Livvy's in with Harley.'

'Fuck!' Roy ran his hands through his hair. 'That's all we need. Okay, don't worry, we won't cause a scene. Grab yourself a break and a coffee. I'll be here for the next couple of hours.'

'Thanks,' Jack said. 'And good luck, Roy.'

18

Roy took a deep breath and opened the door. Livvy didn't even turn around. He assumed she thought it was Jack coming back. He made for the chair Jack had vacated. She looked up and for a minute he saw a flicker of something in her eyes. Fear? Contempt? Who knew? 'Hello, Olivia.' He nodded.

'Oh, hi, erm, Roy,' she stuttered. 'Err, how's things?'

'By things, I assume you mean the boys?'

'Well – yes, of course.' She let go of Harley's hand and got to her feet. 'Are they okay? Have they asked for me?'

'Yes, they have. But they're fine. They're in nursery today.'

'Can I see them sometime? I got a letter from my lawyer, saying they're to live with you until we go to court, but I can have supervised access.'

He was quiet for a moment. She could, but he'd been hoping she wouldn't ask so soon. 'We'll bring them over on Sunday and we'll be staying.'

'There's no need,' she began. 'My parents are here for two weeks – they can supervise.'

'Are you having a laugh? There's every need. After last week's stunt do you honestly think I'd trust you alone with them, parents or no parents? We'll stay a couple of hours. It's the best offer. Take it or leave it.'

She slumped down on the chair, looking defeated. 'I guess I've no choice.'

He nodded. A noise from Harley distracted him. He got to his feet and stroked her hair from her face as she opened her eyes. 'Hello, princess. How you feeling? Would you like a drink?' He helped her to a sitting position and motioned for Livvy to adjust the pillows. He lifted the lidded beaker to Harley's lips and saw Livvy's eyes fill as their daughter sipped like a baby. He swallowed hard to stop any tears – no way would he show any shared emotion with the woman. 'There's my girl. You had enough?' he said as Harley pushed his hand away. 'What, darling?'

'Jack,' she said, looking towards the door.

'I sent him to have some lunch. He needed it, and see, your mom's here now to talk to you.' He sat back and let Livvy get closer to the bed. He watched as Harley waved her right hand around in an effort to communicate. Her speech was slurred and her words slightly jumbled. The left side of her mouth still drooped, although there'd been an improvement in the last few days. Livvy did most of the talking, telling Harley her grandparents would be coming in to see her maybe tomorrow after they'd been to see the babies at Jess's.

Roy closed his eyes and let his thoughts wander. He tried to picture a time in the future when all would be well. Hard to imagine now, but surely things would get better? If only he could turn back time and wipe out all the chaos he'd caused. But then he wouldn't have Harley and the boys and he loved them more than life itself. He was luckier than most men who had affairs. At least he'd got his wife back and she still loved him, despite the odd blip now and again, like the gold stud episode. Livvy hadn't even apologised for entering their home, or for taking the boys. Not a call, nothing and no remorse either by the look of her smiling face now. He must have been scowling because she looked at him and frowned.

'It's okay, Roy. I know this is hard for you. I'm leaving now.' She got to her feet and gave Harley a kiss. 'I'll be back on Saturday, sweetie, and I'll bring Granny and Grandpa. Maybe they'll let us take you for a walk around the grounds if it's fine. Will they allow that, Roy?'

'Yes.' He nodded towards a plush wheelchair in the corner of the room. 'I had that delivered yesterday. Bit more comfortable than hospital issue. If Harley feels up to it, I'm sure she'd enjoy going outside. She's tired today because she's had a physiotherapy session this morning. Soon have you back on your feet though, won't we, princess?'

Harley smiled lopsidedly.

'I'll just see your mom out,' he said and, grabbing her by the elbow, guided Livvy towards the door. In the corridor she shook his hand off and turned to face him.

'No need to practically push me out of the room,' she began. 'What *is* your problem?'

He stared at her and shook his head. 'You really need to ask me that?'

She looked away and then back with a hint of defiance in her eyes. 'You've got everything you want,' she spat. 'You've left me with nothing. You're all so damn smug, you, Sammy, Jane, Eddie, Jon and Jess. Well, don't forget, *I* know about the skeletons in your closets. None of you are any better than me.' She turned to walk away and then, over her shoulder, said, 'Call me about bringing the boys on Sunday. We need to fix a time. I'd better not call *you*. Wouldn't want to upset your precious Sammy now, would we?'

He clenched his fists as she sashayed away, high-heeled boots tapping on the floor, skinny jeans clinging to her pert arse. He shook his head. He could slap her one, but she wasn't worth doing time over. It was hard work biting his tongue though; he could so easily have given her a mouthful. And what skeletons was she on about? None of them had anything to hide. The press had made sure of that in the past.

'Stupid bitch,' he muttered and went back to Harley.

* * *

Livvy took her camera from her handbag and photographed her parents holding their great-grandchildren. They looked so proud; she had to swallow hard to rid herself of the lump in her throat. Her dad looked more relaxed than he'd been in the last few days and at least he was speaking to her again as though he'd forgiven her.

'They both look like Harley,' her mum said, stroking Molly's cheek. 'So dark like proper little Cantellos, I can't see Jack at all.'

Her dad nodded his agreement as Jess came in with a tray of mugs. 'Pop them in their cribs while you have your drinks,' she said, placing the tray on the coffee table. 'Shout out if you need me. I'll be in the utility room sorting laundry. You wouldn't believe how much washing two little mites can make.'

Livvy looked at Jess, who was glowing with contentment as she bent to tickle Ben under his chin. She was still beautiful with her long dark hair, big blue eyes and slender waistline. She felt jealous at the thought of her spending so much time with their grandchildren when *she* couldn't. 'So, you're coping okay, Jess?' She pushed the bitter feelings away in an effort to show interest.

'Oh yes, me and Jon take turns in the night at feeding so that Jack can get some sleep. Poor lad's exhausted, trying to keep up with his uni work and visits to Harley.'

'Jon's pulling his weight, is he?'

'Yes, he's great, he's a really proud grandpa. I'm not saying he won't be having a crafty snooze in the staffroom at work now and again, mind!' Jess laughed and excused herself.

Livvy relaxed back on the sofa with a mug of coffee and her thoughts. All this happy family stuff was nauseating. The babies were lovely, but she felt detached somehow, unable to bill and coo like everyone else. Maybe it was because her boys weren't around and her mothering feelings were suppressed, but even so, she felt angry at being left out of something she should be a big part of. She'd offered to come over and help, but Jess had said she was managing and maybe she could pop in for a visit again next week. It was so obvious that no one wanted her around.

* * *

Back at Ashlea Grange, Livvy felt restless. Her parents were up in their bedroom and Hank was busy preparing vegetables for an early dinner. She looked at her watch: ten to five. The boys would be finishing nursery soon. She grabbed her handbag and car keys – 'Just popping out for a minute.' She dashed out to the car before she changed her mind.

She stopped down the road on the opposite side to the nursery. Sammy's car was already there, parked outside the gates. She ducked low in her seat and put on her shades. Within minutes the gates opened and Sammy and the boys came out. Livvy's stomach churned. She shouldn't be here. If Sammy saw her and reported back to Roy, it would go against her case, but she couldn't wait until Sunday to see them. She needed reassurance that they were okay. They were clutching little red bags, sporting the nursery logo. Danny was chattering away to Sammy while RJ held onto her hand, smiling. They looked happy enough. Sammy opened the car doors and helped them in. She got in herself and Livvy ducked lower as she drove past. She doubted Sammy recognised her registration number as the car was fairly new and, anyway, she'd had her eyes on the road. She felt slightly better for seeing her boys as she drove home.

* * *

'Wow, Nathan, that was brilliant!' Roy said as The Raiders finished their own rousing version of the rock classic 'Summertime Blues'. They were in the studio that Roy had hired for Saturday afternoon's rehearsal, the first with Nathan taking Phil's place on rhythm guitar. Phil was perched on a stool, sitting out the last two songs.

'Whatcha think, Phil?' Eddie said. 'Are you happy to let him stand in for some of the gigs?'

'More than happy,' Phil replied. 'He's bloody brilliant! I might as well take early retirement now.' He grinned good-naturedly as Nathan slugged water from a bottle.

'Tim, Carl? You two happy?' Roy asked as Tim stood his bass guitar on a stand and Carl leant on top of the piano.

'I think we're extremely lucky,' Tim said as Carl nodded his agreement. 'We'd be struggling to do the tour without him.'

Nathan blushed and grinned. 'Thanks, guys. So, I'm in, am I?'

'I think we can safely say you are, mate,' Eddie said, smiling proudly at his grandson.

'Thanks, Pops, and you too, Roy, for the opportunity. Thanks, all of you. I'm really grateful and I can't wait for the tour to begin.'

'You gotta learn to duck-walk for the Chuck Berry covers,' Phil said. 'I doubt Roy can still do it, he struggled on the last tour. But the audience expects it now after so long.'

'I can duck-walk, no problem,' Nathan said, giving them a demonstration.

Roy laughed. 'I'm looking forward to having young blood around. Keep us old buggers on our toes a bit.'

'Another thing,' Phil said, 'he'll be getting all the birds. One look at him and us lot won't stand a chance.'

'Never say never, Phil, eh?' Roy laughed. 'Since when have you ever failed to pull on any tour?'

'Haven't got the energy these days,' he said with a loud sigh.

'Coffees all round?' Eddie asked. 'I'll go to the machine.'

'I'll come with you, Ed.' Roy put down his guitar and followed him out of the studio.

'I'm really impressed with Nathan,' Roy said as they stood by while the vending machine spluttered coffee into plastic cups. 'He's come on a treat since I last heard him play. I mean, he's always been good, but bloody hell, he should be fronting his own band!'

'I think that's his intention eventually,' Eddie said, placing the cups on a tray. 'Coming out with us will be a good grounding for him, sort of like an apprenticeship. I gave him some of our tapes and he's been driving Jess nuts playing along to them. He got sent over to ours last night after waking up the twins and he spent hours in the music room. How's Harley, by the way?'

'Not seen her today. I'll go in tonight. She was doing okay yesterday. As soon as her arm gets a bit stronger, they'll have her up trying a walking frame. Bloody Livvy was there yesterday when I arrived.'

Eddie raised his eyebrows. 'I suppose it's inevitable.'

'I know, but it took me by surprise. Wasn't expecting her. She never thinks to call and make arrangements. Anyway, she's taking her parents in this afternoon. Got to take the kids to Ashlea Grange tomorrow. Not looking forward to it and neither is Sam, but we've no choice. It's either do it amicably or we'll have to go to one of those family mediation centres. I'm not subjecting them to that. We're staying for the visit – can't leave them alone with her.'

'Won't Hank and her folks be there?'

'Hank flies back to LA later. She's already done one disappearing act under her parents' nose. I don't trust her.'

'Fair enough. But if you change your mind and decide to leave them, come over to us for a while.'

Roy sighed. 'I'll see what Sammy says. Right, let's get back to the lads and have another session. I'm really enjoying myself this afternoon. First time I've felt enthusiastic about anything for days.'

* * *

After visiting Harley at the hospital, Livvy dropped her parents in Wilmslow town centre for a shopping spree. Hank would be on his way to the airport by now. They'd already said a stilted goodbye and he'd promised to call her tomorrow. She didn't feel like going home just yet.

She drove aimlessly around for ten minutes, realising how lonely her life was and how lost she'd feel when her mum and dad went home. She might as well be in the States with Hank, *if* he still wanted her. No point in hanging around on her own with no kids to look after and no friends to invite round. She passed a road sign and saw she was on the new stretch of the A34 bypass heading towards Manchester. Hmm, she might as well go and visit Jon and Sean in Flanagan and Grey's for an hour.

* * *

Jon looked up as Livvy ran up the stairs to the record department where he worked.

He greeted her with a hug. 'Hey, hello. What're you doing here?'

'Had a bit of time to kill so thought I'd pop into my old stomping ground and catch up. Sean not around?'

'He's taken the afternoon off. Gone to a wedding, somebody Tina knows from her keep-fit class. Fancy a coffee?'

'No, I'm fine, thanks.' Livvy took a seat on one of a pair of old stools behind the counter. 'So, what have you been up to?'

'Not much, it's one long round of baby-feeding and changing at the mo for me and Jess.'

'I know, she told me. They're doing well, the babies. Seem contented enough.'

'Well, that's down to Jess, Mum and Sammy.'

Livvy nodded.

'What about you? How are things with Hank?'

She shrugged. 'He's gone back to LA today.'

Jon frowned. 'Why didn't you go with him?'

'I can't – I won't see the boys if I do that. Maybe in time, depending what happens with the custody case.'

'Hmm, not good, is it? You should be with Hank. The boys will be fine until things are sorted. Staying on your own in that big old house won't be much fun.'

'I'm going nowhere. Everybody would just love it if I cleared off for good. There's Harley too and the babies. It would help if Jess allowed me to do my bit in taking care of them. She wouldn't hear of it when I offered. It's not fair that Sammy has more access to my flesh and blood than I do.'

Jon stared at her. She looked edgy, twitchy almost, like she was spoiling for a fight. Well, he wasn't getting drawn into anything. A customer approached and handed over two CD cases. Jon busied himself serving while pondering his reply. He said goodbye to the man and turned back to Livvy.

'Look, I'll have a word with Jess. Maybe she can rearrange the schedule to allow you a full afternoon or something. It's not up to me, but I'll try.'

She smiled in response. 'Well, you *do* owe me a favour,' she said, an odd glint in her eyes.

He stared at her. 'How do you work that one out?'

'Sheena! You gave Roy her number and she really landed me in it. Because of her, Hank doesn't want to know me and I've lost my kids.'

Jon took a step back. 'Hey, hang on a minute. Consider your actions before you start laying the blame on everybody else. Sheena did what she had to. *You* were the one that stole the passports and took the kids without permission. You can't blame Roy or Hank for being angry and upset. I'm sure Hank trusted you and he must feel so betrayed. Think about that before you fling accusations around.'

'And *you* should maybe start to consider *your* actions, Jon. How betrayed would Jess feel if she knew you'd screwed Sheena?'

'You wouldn't?'

'Wouldn't I?' She jumped to her feet and waved goodbye as she ran down the stairs. Jon stared after her and then sat down heavily on the vacated stool, stomach churning, and his head in a whirl.

19

Roy sniffed the air appreciatively as he, Sammy and the boys stepped into the hall of Ashlea Grange. His stomach rumbled as Sunday lunch aromas wafted their way. The lounge door opened and Livvy's father came out to greet them.

'Something smells good,' Roy said as he shook Peter by the hand.

'Now that would be Gina's roast beef and Yorkshires,' Peter said. 'She's been busy all morning and is hoping you'll stay and have lunch with us – I'm sure the boys will be hungry.'

'That's very kind of you,' Sammy said. 'They've brought a packed lunch but they can save it until teatime instead. Are you sure it's not too much trouble?'

'It will be our pleasure,' Peter assured her. He led the way to the spacious lounge. 'Take a seat and I'll bring coffees through. Boys, you know where your toys are. Err, Livvy's upstairs, getting ready,' he finished.

'You okay with that?' Roy asked as Peter left the room. 'I wasn't expecting to be fed.' They'd decided not to take up Eddie's offer of popping over for a visit and leaving the boys – Sammy said it wasn't worth taking a chance.

'Yes, we'll make the most of it. Gina's obviously gone to a lot of trouble. It'd be churlish to refuse and sit here like lemons while they all tuck in. Save *me* cooking later.'

Roy smiled. 'Okay. It's fine by me.' He turned as Danny ran across the room with a fire engine, frowning. 'What's wrong, son?'

'Not nee-narring, Daddy.'

'Let's go and ask Grandpa Peter if he can find us some new batteries.' He got to his feet and Danny ran after him.

RJ called to Sammy and she went across to him. He was stuck in the toy box, jean-clad legs waving in the air.

'What are you looking for, RJ?'

'Car,' RJ said, his face bright red as she righted him.

'Which one? The one like Daddy's?' She stopped as the door opened and Livvy slunk into the room.

RJ squealed and ran towards her. She swept him up and hugged him but he smacked her on the chest and pulled her hair.

'Hey, what's that for? Naughty boy,' she said and put him down.

'You go away,' he yelled. 'Where's Yank?'

'I'm not going anywhere, RJ, and Hank's gone home.'

'RJ, come here,' Sammy said and he ran back to her. 'It's not nice to pull hair, it hurts. Say sorry to Mommy, now.' But RJ hid behind her legs and glared balefully at Livvy, who looked like she could throttle him.

The door opened and Roy walked back in, followed by Danny. He sensed an atmosphere and raised an eyebrow in Sammy's direction. She shrugged.

'RJ just pulled Livvy's hair.'

'Oh, now that's bad,' Roy said. 'What have we told you about pulling hair? Are you going to be a good boy now or do you want to sit on the naughty stair? Granny's made a lovely lunch. You won't be able to eat it sat on the stairs, will you?'

'Sorry.' RJ scowled and plugged his thumb into his mouth.

'Thank you, RJ. Danny?' Livvy held her arms out and Danny ran to her. She dropped to her knees and cuddled him. 'That's better. See, Danny always has lots of cuddles for Mommy,' she directed at RJ.

'RJ's very good at cuddling too, aren't you?' Sammy bent to pick him up. 'He's just a bit boisterous at times.'

Livvy sighed. 'Yes, well, seems you can handle him better than I can.'

Roy changed the subject. It felt awkward enough without getting onto who coped best. 'Your mum's been busy,' he said.

Livvy nodded. 'She's in her element, loves cooking huge meals. Oh, excuse me...' She dug in the pocket of her skin-tight jeans and pulled out her phone, glancing at the screen: 'Hank! Back in a minute.' She left the room but the door to the hall didn't quite catch shut and Roy could hear every word she said. He could hear her clicking up and down on her killer heels as she paced the parquet, her voice rising. That floor would be ruined; he was sick of telling her about it. He got the gist. Something to do with this year's CMA in New York. She came back in, her carefully arranged curls not so tidy, as though she'd run her hand through them.

'Sorry about that.' She squeezed the phone back in her pocket and smoothed her hands down her silk shirt.

Roy nodded, glad Sammy was with him as the top three buttons were open, revealing the lace of her black bra. If she bent over, he was sure her tits would explode from their confines. He could swear she'd had a boob job – she used to be pert but much smaller. She looked more Dolly Parton than ever, all tits and hair! He cleared his throat, aware he was staring: 'Didn't intend to eavesdrop, but I heard you mention the CMA.'

'Yes.' She sighed. 'Hank and I have been asked to present the show this year. I told him I can't accept because I don't know what's happening with the boys yet but he's just opened an email from our manager and they need a reply this week.'

'Well, surely you can still do it,' Sammy said. 'It's really prestigious. We'll be here for the boys, no matter who wins custody.'

'We'll see. But you do realise that if I get custody I'll be moving to LA – for good...' She stopped as her father came in with the promised coffees.

'Ah, hen, you're finished at last. You'd think you were getting ready to do a show instead of hosting two wee laddies.'

'Dad!' Livvy rolled her eyes behind his back.

Peter laughed. 'Sorry, hen.'

Livvy flopped down on the sofa opposite Roy and Sammy as her dad left the room.

'Boys, Grandpa's brought you some juice,' Roy said as they jostled to climb on his knee. He pulled a large beanbag forward and made them sit still while they had their drinks.

Livvy's phone rang again and she stared at the screen. Roy saw a faint flush creep up her neck and a slight smirk twisted her glossy lips.

'Sheena,' she said and rejected the call.

Roy frowned. 'Why didn't you take it?'

She shrugged. 'Not the time and place.' She picked up a mug and took a sip of coffee.

Roy stared at her. What was she up to? He felt a dig in his side. Sammy was staring at him, her eyebrows raised in question. He shook his head slightly. The phone rang again and this time Livvy turned it off.

'She can wait. My boys come first.'

* * *

'What did you make of that?' Sammy said as they drove away from Ashlea Grange. 'Her rejecting Sheena's calls, I mean.'

'Dunno, maybe they've fallen out over the phone number saga.'

'Hmm, maybe. There's something going on there. I feel it in my water. Christ, I wish she'd go to bloody LA and stay with Hank until things are sorted!'

'So do I, love,' Roy said, overtaking a tractor and trailer carrying a load of manure. 'Jesus, that stinks!' He put his foot down and whizzed up the lane. 'Shall we take the boys to see the babies? We're only five minutes from Jess and Jon's place. We can visit Ed and Jane at the same time.'

'Yeah, good idea. Boys,' she said, turning to look at them in the back of the car, 'we're going to see the new babies. Now you're Uncle RJ,' she said, pointing at him, 'and you're Uncle Danny.' They grinned at her and nodded. 'Wow, that means you're such big boys now.'

Roy smiled at her. 'You're so good with them, so natural. It's hard not to make comparisons with you-know-who. She just doesn't have the patience, especially with RJ. That bothers me. If it wasn't for Gina and Peter, the visit would have been a disaster. Livvy wasn't interested in the kids after the first ten minutes.'

Sammy nodded. 'Tell me about it. The whole thing was more an exercise of exposing as much flesh and wiggling her arse in your direction every time she bent over. She'll break her bloody neck in those shoes one of these days! Oh, Roy, whatever did you see in her?'

He shrugged. 'God knows, Sam. But let's not go there, eh?' He reached for her hand and squeezed it.

* * *

Sammy smiled as RJ and Danny sat back on the sofa in Jon and Jess's lounge, each with a baby on their knee. 'Jess, have you got your camera handy?' she called. 'They all look so cute.'

Jess, looking harassed, popped her head around the lounge door. 'I was just lifting the chicken out of the oven. The camera's on the dresser over there. Aw, bless them – little uncles!'

Sammy took a few shots. 'Harley will love those,' she muttered to herself. She was worried that Harley still didn't want to see the twins. Regular photos were all they could do at the moment. She looked up as Roy came into the room; he'd been outside for a smoke with Jon.

'Okay, love? Boys, what do you think of the babies?'

'You have it, Daddy,' RJ said, wrinkling his nose at Molly, who was snuffling and chomping on her fingers.

'Are you worried she might start eating you, son?' Roy said, lifting his tiny granddaughter off RJ's lap. 'Are they hungry?'

'Probably,' Sammy said. 'I'll go and get the bottles and you can give Molly hers.' In the kitchen, Jess was draining potatoes over the sink. 'Where's Jon? You could use a hand in here.'

'He went outside for a ciggie with Roy.'

'Well, Roy's back indoors. I assumed Jon was in here with you. We'll feed the babies.'

'Oh, Sam, you arrived just at the right time. There's never enough pairs of hands. The bottles are on the table in jugs of water – they should be the right temperature now.' Jess went to the back door and yelled, 'Jon, get your arse in here! I need some help.' She came back in, shaking her head. 'God knows where he's sloped off to. Oh look, and here's another one who's never around when I need him. Morning, son,' she greeted Nathan, who appeared in the kitchen, yawning and wearing a T-shirt and boxer shorts, his dark curls sticking out at all angles.

'I need a black coffee.' Nathan yawned. 'And don't shout, I've got a headache.'

'You shouldn't drink so much. I hope you didn't get Jack too drunk, he had to be up early to see Harley this morning.'

'He's far too sensible to get rat-arsed!' Nathan grinned.

'Can't have two piss artists in the family, Mother. You'd never cope.'

Jess sighed. 'And to think that once upon a time you were as lovely and innocent as those little souls in the lounge.'

Sammy laughed and took the bottles through. She fastened bibs under the babies' chins and handed Roy a bottle. 'Just pop it in her mouth and Molly will do the rest,' she said. She watched, a lump in her throat, as he gazed besottedly at Molly, who was so like Harley used to be. It took her right back to those happy Livvy-free days that felt like a lifetime ago.

* * *

Livvy switched her phone back on and it beeped with voicemail messages and missed calls. Two from Hank, three from Sheena and two from Jon. She smiled as she listened to Sheena and Jon's messages, both of them begging her to get in touch. They were freaking out big-time. Well, good! Why should *they* be happy when she wasn't? She enjoyed the feeling of power it gave her. She dialled Sheena, who answered immediately.

'Livvy, what the hell are you playing at? I've been trying to call you all day.'

'Sorry, I had Roy and our boys over for lunch.' She left out that Sammy and her parents were also there too. It hardly mattered. She'd sat opposite Roy at the table and he'd been unable to take his eyes off her cleavage. Her fantastic new bra with extra push-up certainly did the trick – she must order more.

'Roy? For lunch? What's going on then? Are your parents still down there?'

'Err, yes, they are. Mum cooked for us.'

'Oh, right. Anyway, what are you trying to do to Jon? He called me in a right state. Said you'd been to see him. He's convinced you're going to tell Jess about our fling.'

'Is he? Don't know where he gets that idea from.' She grinned into the receiver.

'You. He got it from you. Why are you being such a cow about this? Don't you think he and Jess have enough on their plates at the moment?'

'No more than me, Sheena. I've got a sick daughter, an absent husband and those babies are my grandchildren too.'

'That's all the more reason to stop this pissing about then. Jess is doing her best to care for the twins. The last thing she needs is you trying to destroy her marriage.'

'I'm not. Jon's fixing it for me to help her a bit more. Don't know why you're getting all worked up, Sheena. It's really got nothing to do with you.'

'Nothing to do with me? Well, there's my marriage that could be wrecked too. Or don't you care? All Gerry and I have done is support you. I even found your father for you. I can't believe you're being so horrible. What the hell's happened to you, Livvy?'

Livvy ended the call without a goodbye. She lay back on her bed. Next, she called Jon, but his phone went straight through to the message service. She left him a message, asking him to call her as soon as possible.

* * *

Jon heard Jess calling and turning his phone off, went back inside. Livvy wasn't answering his calls or texts. He'd spoken to Sheena to warn her and she'd said she wasn't really surprised. He felt sick thinking about what might be on the cards for him. The whole family could be destroyed. His dad and Jane would disown him. Jess would probably throw him out. He couldn't understand why Livvy was being so evil. They'd always been good pals when they'd worked together years ago. His dad had been supportive of her and Jane had even delivered Harley when Livvy went into labour unexpectedly. It was almost like she'd had a personality transplant and was hell-bent on alienating them all. And now he had to try and persuade Jess to let her come round more often to help with the twins and all the while wondering if she'd say anything to land him in the shit. But if he didn't ask, she'd do it anyway so he couldn't win. Bitch!

20

'Boys, come and sit at the table and make a nice welcome-home card for your sister.' Sammy set out crayons and a pile of paper and stickers on the kitchen table. 'Daddy and Jack have gone to bring Harley home from the hospital.'

'Got glue, Sammy?' Danny asked, looking hopeful.

'Me wants glitter,' RJ added.

'Okay, but don't get it all over the place.' Sammy handed a little basket of craft stuff to Danny. 'Stay at the table with it, and RJ, no sprinkling it in Danny's hair.' She smiled, recalling the time they'd made a card for Roy's birthday. It had taken forever to wash the glitter and glue out of their hair and clothes. She and Roy were still finding it weeks later on worktops, in crevices and even in the butter. 'I'm just going upstairs to give Mrs Melcher a hand to get Harley's room ready. Be good.'

Mrs Melcher was busy re-arranging the furniture in Harley's old bedroom. 'I've pushed that big recliner chair over by the window so she can sit and look out at the garden if the fancy takes her,' she said as Sammy walked into the bedroom.

'Good idea,' Sammy said, tweaking the decorative cushions on the bed into place. 'It looks fine there. And there's still plenty of room to walk around. Is that new seat in place in the bathroom?'

'Yes, I've fixed it over the bath. Just make sure it's secure before she sits on it. And the frame for around the toilet's in there too.'

Sammy nodded, feeling close to tears. This was ridiculous. Harley was a young woman with all her life ahead of her and they were equipping her room as though she were an elderly lady on her last legs. She hurried into the en suite and fiddled with the towels on the rail. There'd be carers coming in early mornings to get her up and bathed. Roy had insisted that they could manage, but the hospital would only discharge Harley on the grounds that he and Sammy employed professional help. Harley needed to be lifted in a proper manner to prevent injury, they said. Her physiotherapist would be coming three times a week, so at Roy's expense, one of the smaller bedrooms had been fitted with specialist gym equipment. Sammy felt she'd make a quicker recovery with all the family and familiar things around her. She was also hoping they'd make a breakthrough in reuniting Harley with her babies, whom she still hadn't seen since the day of her stroke.

'I'll go and see what the little monkeys are up to and put the kettle on,' Sammy said. 'Come and join us when you're ready. Are you staying until Harley gets home?'

'I will, thanks. Then she can tell me if she wants anything in a certain place.'

Sammy nodded. Downstairs, she gave the boys a drink and some biscuits and admired their efforts at producing cards. 'Now try and write your names. Here, see, I'll write them on a piece of paper and you can copy. Don't forget to draw some kisses on the bottom. You can take them up to Harley's bedroom later with Mrs Melcher.'

* * *

Livvy took a seat on the sofa in Jess's lounge. Jess handed her Molly and a bottle. Jane was seated opposite with Ben.

'All hands on deck this morning,' Livvy said, smiling at Jane.

'More or less,' Jane replied, sitting Ben forwards and burping him. 'Sammy's busy getting ready for Harley coming home. Just a pity it's not a nursery day for the boys but I'm sure she'll cope.'

'I could have had the boys,' Livvy said. 'Or at least taken care of them at Jasmine House.' She noticed Jane shoot a look at Jess, who raised an eyebrow and left the room. Livvy knew she'd never be welcome at Sammy's precious Jasmine House and added, 'I'm quite capable of looking after my own children.'

'I'm sure you are,' Jane said. 'But it's a bit of a sensitive subject, don't you think? Anyway, you're helping *us* out and we really appreciate it. I have to leave soon, got a dental appointment. Jess needs you here. Oh, Molly's stopped sucking. You need to wind her. Here...' She passed a white muslin square to Livvy. 'Put that on your shoulder or over your knee. It's best to wear your old clothes for this job, just in case.'

'In case what?'

'In case she pukes. You don't want it on that suede jacket – the stain will never come out. I'd take it off if I were you.'

Livvy nodded. 'I never thought.'

'Right, that's Ben all done,' Jane said. 'I'll pop him down and see if Jess needs any help in the kitchen. Will a sandwich do you for lunch?'

'Err, anything, thanks,' Livvy said, lifting Molly up to her shoulder and grimacing as the baby burped loudly down her ear.

She looked around as Jane left the room. Photos on the walls told of a happy family life. Nathan and Jack as toddlers, their first school portraits, gangly teens in their Manor Banks uniforms. Shots of Jess and Jon, holding each other around the waist and smiling into one another's eyes. A family portrait of

Jane and Eddie, with their four children and the twins. It gave her such a feeling of power to know that she could destroy that family closeness if she chose. The Mellors and Cantellos had everything she'd ever craved. Okay, so she had the music career now and the money and the husband, for what it was worth. She also had the family, but all four children were gone, for now. She had no shared closeness with anyone. And since her parents went home on Monday, she was alone at Ashlea Grange and she hated it. The easiest thing would be to get on a plane, go to Hank and grovel for all she was worth but she hadn't finished here yet and she certainly wasn't done with Roy. He might be play-acting at being the perfect father and husband right now, but she knew his weaknesses. She just needed to bide her time and get him alone, no Sammy and no kids. She was giving no one an easy ride before she left town for good. She knew that Jon would be shitting himself at work right now, wondering if she'd landed him in it yet. She grinned and sent him a quick text, telling him she was sitting on his sofa, waiting for Jess to join her for a chat – that should shoot his blood pressure off the Richter scale.

* * *

Jon looked at his phone as it beeped. He read Livvy's text.

'Problem, Jon?' Sean said. 'You've gone quite pale.'

'Oh, no, it's nothing; just a message trying to sell me something. Car insurance, you know.'

'Oh, right. Do you want to go for your lunch then? Have a stroll around, might wake you up a bit. You look like you haven't slept for ages.'

Jon smiled. 'It's the twins, they're awake every couple of hours for feeding. Don't know how Jess is coping.'

'She has help, doesn't she? Livvy called Tina last night. Said she's going round to yours today to lend a hand.'

'Did she? That all she said?'

'Far as I know. I make myself scarce when anyone calls. Tina can yap for hours. Why do you ask?'

'No reason.' Jon shrugged. 'I'm off, see you in an hour.'

He left the shop, walked to Piccadilly Gardens and sat down on a bench, ignoring the old woman already sitting at the opposite end, sharing her sandwiches with a few pigeons. Dare he call Jess, see how she was doing? She'd think it odd if he didn't as he called her every lunchtime. While he was debating, his phone rang out: Sheena.

'Hi,' he began, 'how you doing?'

'I'm worried. Have you spoken to her yet? She's not picking up on me. I don't know whether to just get it over with and tell Gerry then we can hopefully put it behind us. I can't handle this stress.'

Jon sat forward and took a deep breath. 'For God's sake, don't do that. Livvy might just be winding us up – you know, enjoying a power trip. What's the point in saying anything until we have to? I know how you feel because it's making me ill, worrying like this. I can't sleep and I can't eat, but to have Jess find out would be the end for us. I can't lose her. Please, Sheena. Keep it to yourself for now.'

He heard her sigh and then, 'Okay, Jon. But try and talk to Livvy as soon as you can.'

'Easier said than done. She's at my place with Jess right now, helping with the twins. That's part of her blackmailing me. She made me promise to ask Jess if she could help. Jess didn't want her there too often and I had to beg her. I'm sick with fear that she'll say something today. She sent me a snide little text earlier, letting me know she was sitting in my house – like a warning.'

'She's a bitch.'

'You don't need to tell *me*. I'll call you if I have any news.

Take care.' He ended the call and leant his head back, staring up at the cloudless blue sky.

* * *

Jess put down her coffee mug and picked up the phone. 'Hi, darling. How you doing? Thought you weren't bothering calling me today. You're later than usual. No, they're both flat out. Livvy's here, she's been a great help. Good suggestion of yours to rope her in.' She smiled at Livvy, who smiled back. 'We're just having our lunch and then she has to go. Okay, well I'll see you later. Love you too, babes.' She hung up. 'Poor Jon, he's knackered. We could do with a few days away, just the two of us.'

'A second honeymoon?' Livvy suggested.

'Now that would be nice seeing as we hardly had a first. Two days in Paris while Mum and Dad looked after the boys. Ah well, I can dream.'

'You and Jon are very lucky. At least you've still got each other.'

'Yep, I guess we are. I love him more now than I ever did,' Jess said. 'And he tells me he feels the same.'

'And at least you know you can trust him. Jon's not the type to stray. Not like Roy.' Livvy almost choked on his name.

Jess looked at her. 'You okay? Something go down the wrong way?'

Livvy picked up her coffee mug and took a sip.

Jess continued, 'I know Jon would never cheat on me. And really, you know, Roy's very settled with Sammy. They're so happy. It all worked out well in the end. I'm sure once you sort things out with Hank, you'll be fine. It's just such a shame about Harley, but she'll get the best help money can buy if it's anything to do with Roy.'

* * *

On the way home from Jess's, Livvy stopped off at the supermarket and bought a couple of ready prepared pasta meals, red wine and a bottle of vodka. She drove home in contemplative silence, not even bothering to turn on the radio. She felt consumed with anger towards everyone. Jon would be driving home from work soon to Jess and they'd sit together enjoying a meal and maybe a glass of wine. They'd relax and watch TV or maybe a DVD once the babies were settled. They'd have a cuddle and then he would suggest they go to bed and not for a sleep and Jess would agree. She shook her head. He didn't deserve her – Jess was too good for him. Over at the Cantellos, once the boys were asleep and Harley settled, a similar scenario would be played out. Thoughts of Roy screwing Sammy made her feel sick. She looked at the clock on the dash: five fifteen. Early, but she needed a drink – and quick. She gripped the steering wheel and put her foot down.

* * *

Roy smiled and called out to Sammy to come to Harley's room. His daughter lay on her bed propped up on pillows and on each side of her, a little brother lay snuggled close.

'You boys keeping your big sister warm?' he asked, tickling RJ, who squirmed away from him, giggling.

Harley nodded. 'They're cuddly,' she managed to say.

'Hey, listen to you,' Sammy said, coming into the room. 'Your speech is really improving. Well done, sweetheart.'

Harley waved her right arm. 'Babies, tomorrow.'

Roy grinned. 'You wanna see the babies tomorrow? Really, do you?'

Harley nodded. 'Yes. With Jack.'

'Oh, princess, of course.' He choked on his tears.

'Me hungry,' Danny announced, rubbing his tummy.

'I'll take them to McDonald's,' Sammy said. 'Can you make Harley a bite to eat, Roy? Do you fancy some scrambled eggs, darling?'

She nodded.

'Dad will make them for you while I take these two out for an hour. They've been cooped up all day so it'll help tire them out.'

* * *

Jon drove home with a heavy heart. He'd had another text from Livvy half an hour earlier, saying,

Your secret's safe with me – for now!

Why the fuck was she doing this? What had he and Sheena ever done to hurt her? He'd a good mind to go over to Ashlea Grange later and belt the hell out of her, but what good would it do? He'd get done for assault and then it would all come out. All he could do for now was go with the flow and hope she was bluffing, just because she could. He pulled up outside his barn conversion bungalow on his dad's land and clambered out. Jess was sitting on the front doorstep, smoking a crafty fag. He smiled and waved. She waved back, a big grin splitting her face as though glad to see him – so far, so good. She'd given up smoking ages ago, but had the occasional social smoke; she must be feeling a bit frazzled with the babies to be succumbing now.

* * *

Livvy finished her macaroni cheese and poured a third glass of red wine. She felt a bit more chilled now and took her wine into the lounge. She dialled Jasmine House and Roy answered. She told him she was coming to visit Harley later – she had some-thing to do first but would be there within the hour. Before he had time to answer, she cut him off. He called her back, but she rejected his call. She wasn't prepared to listen to him telling her to stay away. He had three of her kids under his roof. As far as she was concerned that gave her more rights than Sammy had. She finished her drink and went upstairs to get ready. A quick shower, fresh make-up, hair fluffed out so that it fell in a mass of soft curls around her face. Black lacy underwear, short denim skirt and tight-fitting top with a low-cut neckline... her high-heeled sandals completed the look. She grabbed her handbag and keys, went back into the lounge and poured a large vodka, downing it almost in one go, then re-did her lip gloss. She took a deep breath and felt ready to go.

21

Livvy swung the car through the open gates of Jasmine House, swerved up the long gravel drive and just missed the edge of the manicured lawn. The wine and vodka combo had kicked in more than she'd anticipated but she figured adrenaline played a big part in her feeling high, too. She pulled up outside the garage block next to Roy's BMW and her heart pounded as she realised Sammy's car was missing. Perfect.

She cut the engine, sat back in the seat for a minute and closed her eyes, then opened them again as her head started to whirl. She took a deep breath, rummaged in the glove compartment for her minty mouth spray, re-did her lip gloss, fluffed out her curls and glanced in the vanity mirror: the glow in her cheeks enhanced her looks. Satisfied, she got out of the car and carefully picked her way across the gravel to the front door. One false move in these heels and she'd go arse over tit. Not quite the cool impression she wanted to make. Roy was going to pay her some attention tonight, whether he liked it or not. She rang the doorbell and stood slightly back.

Roy opened the door, a look of disgust on his face. She ignored it and batted her lashes at him as he told her to come in.

He slammed the door shut and walked away. She followed him into the kitchen and looked around.

'Where are RJ and Danny?'

'Out for tea with Sammy.'

She tutted. 'Bad planning, I could have seen all my kids together.'

'Tough,' Roy said. '*We* didn't know you were coming. If you hadn't hung up on me, I'd have told you to wait until they were all here. Anyway, the sooner you have your visit with Harley, the better as far as I'm concerned. I'll show you to her room.'

'I know where her room is, Roy.' She made to walk to the door.

'There's no way you're snooping about on your own – look at the damage you did last time.'

Livvy stared at him and then headed out of the kitchen with Roy on her heels. She climbed the stairs, him following, knowing that he'd have no choice but to look up her skirt and at her legs. She reached the landing and turned to him: 'Look, Roy, I'm truly sorry about what I did. I needed to be with Hank. I was trying to save my marriage. Please, just give me half an hour alone with Harley. If you're standing over my shoulder, there'll be tension and we don't want to upset her, now do we?'

Roy huffed. 'Okay, you have a point. Ten minutes though, that's all you get. She's tired and needs her rest – doctor's orders.'

'Fair enough.' Livvy smiled and went into Harley's room, feeling his eyes boring into her back.

* * *

Roy stubbed out his cigarette on the patio and went back inside. He paced the living room, glass of single malt in hand, surprised to feel his teeth chattering. That bloody woman reduced his nerves to shreds. He needed Sammy here; he wished she'd hurry up. He'd expected them back by now. How long did it take two kids to eat a Happy Meal? Mind you, the way Danny dawdled with his food they could be ages. Then again, it was late-night opening, Toys R Us was on the same block as McDonald's and knowing the kids, he'd bet his life they'd persuaded her to take them in for a treat. He poured another drink and stood by the patio window. The bronze sculpture of him and Sammy seemed to be watching him. He looked at his watch: she'd had more than ten minutes. He put his glass down on the fireplace and made towards the stairs to call time, but he heard a door closing as he reached the bottom step.

Livvy appeared on the landing and the fading sunlight coming through the stained-glass windows threw up highlights in her hair. Her cheeks were flushed and her lips looked fresh and glossy. He caught himself staring, her short skirt showing off lightly tanned legs, her low-cut top accentuating her cleavage and the lacy top of her black bra.

She smiled and sashayed down the stairs towards him. 'Thank you for that,' she said.

He nodded. 'You'd better go now.' There was a glint in her eyes and he knew it well. He turned away as she came towards him. He felt sick, he just wanted her out of the house.

'Could I have five minutes, Roy? I'd like to discuss the boys.'

He felt his heart thumping as she came closer and wished he hadn't had the whisky.

Livvy chewed her lip. 'Is that whisky I can smell on your breath? How about one for old time's sake while we talk about the boys? What I have to say will only take five minutes and I could really use a drink.'

Roy stared at her. Maybe she'd tell him she was going to LA and he could have custody of the kids after all. 'Five minutes,' he said, leading the way into the lounge. His hand shook as he picked up his drink and went to stand behind the sofa. For some daft reason he felt safer there.

Livvy moved into the room and stood on the rug in front of the fire. 'Do I have to help myself?'

'What?'

'A drink. Please.'

He shook his head. 'Just say what you have to say. No drink.'

She sighed. 'For God's sake, I won't bite you. One drink, please.'

He went to the drinks cabinet, downed his in one go and poured himself another large measure and a single one for her. He picked up the drinks and turned, almost dropping the glasses. She had her back to him, facing the fireplace, and was stepping out of her skirt.

'What the fuck are you doing?'

'One for old time's sake, Roy.' She took off her top, still with her back to him, and let it drop to the floor.

Roy stared, open-mouthed. 'No way! Get the fuck out of my house.' He could feel his chest getting tight and took a deep breath. Sammy would be back any minute with the kids. She'd go ballistic; she'd never believe this wasn't his doing.

Livvy turned to face him and hooked her thumbs in the sides of her black lacy thong, sliding it slowly over her hips and down her thighs. She kicked it towards him. It sailed past his nose. Roy stood still, unable to move as she undid her bra and threw it towards the statue of him and Sammy, where it landed on the top of his sculptured head. She strode up to him, naked, and took the drinks, knocking them both back. She dropped the empty glasses onto the sofa and swayed rhythmically in front of him, running her hands up and down her body and swishing her curls around.

'I bet I can still turn you on.' She laughed. 'You don't need to hide it from me. Would you like me to dance for you?' she said, stroking her breasts. 'Come on, you know you want me one last time. We always had such fun in bed. You could never get enough of me.' She reached to unzip him but he smacked her hands away. 'Roy, come on, you can't fight this, *you* know you're horny, *I* know you're horny. What are we waiting for? I know you want me.'

'Not a chance in hell,' he said. 'Get dressed and get out of my house.'

She danced away from him and lay down on the rug where only last night he'd made love to Sammy. His stomach turned over at the sight of her spreading her legs.

'No one need ever know,' she said, stroking herself between her thighs. 'Come on, I won't tell Sammy. Come and do it for me. I don't want to pleasure myself. You know what I like better than anyone else does.'

'You need to go,' Roy said, running his hands through his hair. He gathered up her clothes and threw them at her. 'You're mad – or pissed – or both. Just get out.'

She sat up and stared at him. 'You don't mean that, you know you don't.'

'Leave!' Her stare was unnerving him. Her eyes looked wild. He felt like picking her up bodily and throwing her out, but he didn't want to touch her.

She got to her feet, tears in her eyes. 'Roy,' she said softly and walked towards him. 'You know you want me.' She held her breasts and pushed them upwards. 'Look, you love them, don't you? I saw you looking at them on Sunday. You couldn't take your eyes off them. Remember what you always used to say? Nipples like raspberries. I'm still pert, even after all these years. Please, Roy, if you're not going to love me then at least give me one last cuddle. You might like it and if you do then we could get married in time. I'll divorce Hank and you can easily get rid of Sammy. Then we can bring up the boys together, just like we planned before. No need for custody battles. Just you, me and our children. We could be really happy, if you'd just give us another chance. So come on, what harm can a cuddle do?'

Roy felt frozen to the spot. The angry words he wanted to yell wouldn't leave his mouth and before he could make a move, she flung her arms around his neck and pulled his face down to hers. As her lips met his, he came to his senses and jerked backwards, falling onto the sofa with Livvy straddling him and clinging to him.

'Get off me, you bitch!' he yelled and grabbed her around the neck, trying to force her off his lap. 'Just get off me, you evil cow!'

'Royyyyyyyyyyyyyyy!'

Livvy stopped struggling and turned towards the sound. Roy froze and looked to the door, where Sammy was standing open-mouthed with the boys just behind her.

Livvy threw back her head and started to laugh. Roy tried to push her away again but she clung on, laughing hysterically.

'Oh my God, the kids!' Sammy turned and bundled them out of the room, slamming the door behind her.

Roy pushed Livvy so hard that she fell backwards onto the floor. He jumped up and yanked her to her feet, shaking her as Sammy came back into the room.

'I've had to shut the kids in the utility room, for God's sake. What the hell's happening here?'

'Ah, Sammy, your wonderful husband and I had one last fuck for old time's sake,' Livvy said, slurring a little.

She glared at her. 'He's fully clothed. He had his hands around your neck. *You* were attacking him.'

'She's well and truly flipped,' Roy said.

'Get dressed and get out of my home!' Sammy yelled. 'You have one minute!'

'I want to see my boys,' Livvy said and started to cry.

'Not in a million years,' Sammy said. 'And those crocodile tears won't wash with me. Get dressed and Roy will see you to the door.'

'Bitch!' Livvy spat. 'No wonder Roy likes it better with me.

We have such great times. He hates your blow jobs, says you haven't a clue.'

'Don't listen to a word she says, Sam.'

'I've no intention.' Sammy clenched her fists and lunged forwards, smacking Livvy so hard across the face she stumbled and fell, knocking her head on the corner of the coffee table.

Roy grabbed hold of Sammy and held her in his arms as Livvy got to her feet, holding her cheek. 'I'll have you done for assault,' she said, her lips trembling as she gathered up her clothes. She walked towards the door and turned: 'This isn't over yet!'

Roy sat a shaking Sammy down on the sofa and then manhandled Livvy to the front door. He pushed her outside, slammed it shut and locked it. Heart thumping and hands shaking, he went back into the lounge to Sammy.

22

Livvy sat on the doorstep and pulled on her clothes. At least the house was secluded with no close neighbours to see her. She put her hand up to her face. Her cheek was throbbing and her eye felt sore – she'd have a real shiner by tomorrow. All the better for reporting Sammy's assault. It would make good press, maybe even help her custody case, and she'd make sure every newspaper in the land got the details. She sat for a minute or two and got her breath back. She still felt drunk but there was no way she was giving up on seeing her sons. It was getting dark now. She took off her shoes so they didn't crunch the gravel and crept around to the back of the house. Underneath the first window she spotted a tumble-dryer vent in the wall, the utility room, and put her ear against the door. Nothing! Sammy must have got the boys out of there. She slunk towards the kitchen window and saw them sitting at the table by the patio doors – Sammy was pouring them milk.

The kitchen window was open and she could hear Sammy talking to Roy but couldn't tell what they were saying. She gazed at the boys as they munched on biscuits and knew she had to see them. She crept back to the utility room door and tried the handle: it was unlocked. Holding her breath, she slipped inside, looked quickly around and hurried to the far corner, where a laundry basket was piled high with clothes. She slid to the floor, hiding behind the mountain of clothes, taking deep breaths to regain composure. She could hear the boys chattering and giggling and then Sammy telling them it was time for bed and to say goodnight to Daddy.

Livvy waited a few more minutes until she heard Roy asking Sammy if she was ready for a G&T and to come and join him in the lounge. She held her breath as she opened the door leading into the kitchen, praying it wouldn't squeak. She heard Sammy calling out to Roy that she was on her way and then the sound of the lounge door closing. She left her shoes behind, tiptoed through the kitchen on bare feet and went silently up the stairs to the nursery.

The boys were lying quietly, Danny cuddling his old blanket and RJ, thumb in mouth, twiddling his toy bunny's ear. She put her finger to her lips as they stared at her, wide-eyed. 'Shhhh, come with Mommy! We have to pretend we're quiet little mice. I'm going to take you for a very exciting adventure, but we mustn't disturb anyone,' she whispered. She helped them out of bed and put on their slippers and dressing gowns. 'Isn't this fun?' she said as they sneaked out of the bedroom. 'Now we have to be very, very quiet on the stairs so shhh!' She put her finger to her lips again as they crept quietly down the stairs and she stood still in the hall for a second, listening. She heard the low murmur of Roy and Sammy talking and shepherded the boys into the kitchen and through into the utility room. Smiling reassuringly at them, she picked up her shoes as they sneaked out into the cool night air.

* * *

Roy pulled Sammy close as they sat side by side on the sofa. He kissed her and stroked her hair as she sobbed against his chest. She'd done well and held herself together in front of the kids but the shock had knocked her for six. He was thankful Harley had slept through it all.

'You do believe me, Sam, don't you? It wasn't my fault. She didn't give me the chance to tell her not to come. I thought you'd be back before she arrived – I should have called your mobile but I didn't want to spoil the boys' tea.'

'Of course I do,' Sammy said. 'The brazen cheek of the bitch! I couldn't believe what I was walking into, it was so horrible.'

'I'm sure. It was for me too. I think we should ring the police. She's flipped. Who knows what she might do next? Shall I call Hank?'

'And tell him what? He won't want to know her. We need her to go over there to him, not stay around here. She's his wife, it's up to him to sort her out.'

Sammy picked her drink up from the coffee table. She took a sip and jumped as the doorbell rang: 'What if it's her again? Oh no, she might have told the police that I smacked her one.' She stopped as the bell rang again continuously and then someone banged loudly on the front door.

They both got up to answer it. Jon was on the doorstep, looking agitated.

'Come in,' Roy said. 'What's wrong? My God, Jon, you're white as a sheet! What's happened, son?'

Jon held out a bunch of car keys. 'Is *she* meant to have the boys?'

'Who?' Sammy gasped.

'Livvy. She's in the car with them at the bottom of the drive. The gates were open, I just drove straight through.'

'Oh my God!' Roy dashed outside with Sammy, Jon following.

'I saw the keys in the ignition,' Jon said. 'I don't know why I took them, but it felt the right thing to do, then as I'm nearly at your door that bitch came sneaking out from the back of the house with the boys. She ran past me to the car, dragging the kids with her. When she realised I'd got the keys, she locked the doors from inside.'

All three rushed down the drive. Roy pounded on the windows, yelling at Livvy to open the doors. She lay slumped over the wheel, sobbing, ignoring him.

'Open the doors, Livvy. You're going nowhere!' Roy shouted.

'Roy, stop, you're scaring the boys,' Sammy said, peering through the windows. 'They're both crying. Oh, poor little mites! They were all tucked up in bed and nearly asleep when I left them. How could she do this? She's not even got car seats in *and* she's been drinking.'

'Open it, Jon,' Roy said. 'She's had her chance.'

Jon opened the central locking and Roy and Sammy lifted the sobbing boys from the back seat. Sammy hurried them back inside the house.

'I've been kicked out,' Jon said. 'That bitch showed up at the house and told Jess about me and Sheena.'

'Oh my God,' Roy said. 'You're joking?'

'Oh, it gets better,' Jon added, grabbing hold of Livvy and dragging her out of the car. 'She claimed I was screwing *her* too! Needless to say, Jess went berserk.'

'I've heard enough,' Roy said, running his hands through his hair. 'I'm calling the police. You'd better come inside, Jon.'

As Roy and Jon headed up the drive, Livvy screamed after them: 'You're fucking hypocrites, all of you!' She ran up the drive and snatched the keys from Jon's hand.

'And you're just a slut,' he said.

'You've heard nothing yet, mate,' Roy said, glaring at Livvy. 'You should have seen her performance earlier.'

'I'm no slut. I'm not the one who screwed around, yet it's me that gets all the shit!' she yelled. 'It's me that can't have my boys, me that gets all the blame.'

'It's always, me, me, me, with you,' Roy said. 'Time you took responsibility for your own actions. I'm phoning the police. Come on, Jon.'

* * *

Livvy got back in the car and started up the engine. She screeched off the drive, swerving to avoid the gateposts and kicking up gravel with the tyres.

She wiped a hand across her face and put her foot down. She felt angry as she drove in a haze of drink and bitterness; she didn't know where to go, certainly not back to Ashlea Grange, she couldn't handle that. There was nothing else for it but to drive up to Glasgow to her parents' place. She headed for the motorway, thinking about what she'd done. Why the hell had she told Jess? She'd achieved nothing and didn't even feel better for it. She was really in the shit now. Maybe she should drive to Sheena's first and give her a mouthful. After all, it was Sheena's fault. She'd landed her right in it. Why should *she* still be in a so-called happy marriage? Gerry needed to be told the truth about his cheating wife. But no doubt Jess would be telling him soon, if she hadn't already.

Nobody would want to know her now. Nobody understood her, she didn't even understand herself. This was all Roy's fault. If he'd married her when he was supposed to, none of this would have happened. She hated him for not wanting her. How could he have refused to make love to her? She couldn't have made it any plainer that she wanted him. How dare he reject her for the sake of that cow he was married to? One fuck and she could have blown his life apart tonight.

And Jon, the way *he'd* gone on, as though screwing her

wouldn't have been a good thing, even though it was all in her imagination. Who did he think he was? Oh, but the look of horror on Jess's face had been worth it though. She didn't think Jess would ever forgive him. But then again, the whole hypocritical lot of them seemed able to forgive each other's misdemeanours and maybe that's what you did in time if you loved someone enough. She wouldn't know, she'd never had those sorts of feelings, except for Roy. Her life was a screwed-up mess and none of it was her doing. It was all Jon's fault. He was the one who gave Sheena's number to Roy. She'd never get custody now. Her mum would hate what she'd done and her dad would give her the silent treatment, again. She'd let Harley down, hurting Jack's family like that. Hank would definitely want rid of her once he got wind of this little escapade. What sort of a wife was she, stripping off in front of her ex like that?

She did a U-turn and headed back towards Roy's place. She hadn't finished with him yet. She was the victim in all this, thanks to Roy, Sheena and Jon. How she hated them and their smug little lives. They didn't deserve to be happy.

She pulled up on Jasmine Lane, a couple of hundred yards from the gates. A police car blocked the entrance, blue lights flashing hypnotically. Shit, they'd chuck the book at her! She'd lose all her fans. Hank would throw her out of the band. Tears rolled down her cheeks as she revved the engine. She put her foot down and sped towards the police car, closing her eyes just before impact.

* * *

'Attempted kidnap, burglary, sexual assault... These are serious offences, Mr Cantello,' the officer taking notes said. 'We'll bring her in soon enough, but meanwhile you'll have to come down to the station and make a full state—' He stopped as a loud bang and an explosion rattled the windows and shook the walls.

'What the—' Roy began as the policeman made for the front door. Roy, Sammy and Jon followed him outside.

'Oh my God, the cop car's ablaze,' Roy shouted, running down the drive. 'Shit!' He saw Livvy's car on its crushed roof on the driveway. The policeman pushed past him and pulled Livvy free. He lay her on the lawn, shouting into his radio for an ambulance and the fire brigade.

Roy put his arm around Sammy's shoulders and pulled her away. He could tell from the way Livvy's head had fallen back that her neck had snapped and her blue eyes, though empty, stared coldly up at him. He pushed Sammy gently towards Jon who, white-faced, held her while Roy bent double-retching onto the driveway.

23

Roy saw the last of the mourners out and quickly closed the door. The paparazzi were still hanging around outside Ashlea Grange. Hadn't they done enough muckraking in the three weeks since Livvy's death? They'd had a field day, making up half the nonsense they printed. He hated any sort of publicity, had always fought shy and tried to shield his family from press invasion, but there was no getting away from this one. He was sick to the back teeth of muttering 'No comment' every time a mic or camera was thrust in his direction.

He sighed and went back into the lounge. Harley, Jack, Courtney and her partner, Jamie, were huddled up on one of the sofas. On the opposite sofa sat Livvy's parents, Peter and Gina, who looked like they'd aged twenty years, alongside a bereft and lost-looking Hank and two of his teenage daughters, Ariel and Maddi, who'd accompanied him to the UK.

Sammy had stayed home with the little ones – a funeral wasn't the place for kids and they still hadn't told the boys where Mommy had gone. Not that they'd asked for her. They'd been clingy towards Sammy since the night Livvy tried to take them away. Roy and Sammy had kept the events of the night prior to the car crash from Peter and Gina, although they were curious to know why Livvy's best friend Sheena wasn't in attendance at her funeral. Roy told them they needed to call her when they got home – he didn't want to get involved in all that, he had enough to cope with. Hank had insisted they tell him every last detail. He said he had to know what had driven her to such extremes, even though Roy knew it had sickened him to hear the truth.

'Can I get anyone another drink?' Roy strode to the drinks cabinet and poured himself a whisky, gesturing the bottle at the others. 'Or what about a brandy?'

'Me and Gina will have a small brandy, please,' Peter said, his arm around Gina's shoulders. Roy nodded and took their drinks across. He felt sorry for them. They'd only had Livvy back in their lives for a few short years. Thank goodness those years had been better than the last one.

'Hank, can I get you anything?'

He shook his head.

'Jack? Jamie?'

'No, thanks,' Jamie said.

'Not for me, Roy,' Jack said. 'I think I need to get Harley home now, she's had enough for today.'

Roy and Jack helped Harley into her wheelchair. His poor daughter looked wiped out. 'I'll call you a taxi,' Roy said. 'I don't want you driving, Jack – you've had a few drinks. Courtney, why don't you and Jamie go back to Jasmine House with them? Sammy will look after you and *I'll* be back later. I don't think you should stay here on your own tonight.'

Courtney sighed and got to her feet. Roy caught her as she almost passed out. The girl was exhausted. It had taken over a week to track her and Jamie down on their South American travels. She'd finally responded from an internet café, to a frantic email message to call Roy, and then spent a couple more days getting to civilisation and arranging a flight. The funeral had to be put on hold until both of Livvy's daughters could attend. Also, Courtney had had to contend with seeing her sister temporarily disabled by the stroke, something they'd all kept from her while she'd been on the other side of the world.

'What about you and Gina, Peter? Do you want me to get you a cab back to the Grand? And Hank and the girls?' Roy had booked them all into the Wilmslow hotel. He felt they'd be more comfortable there than rattling around in this place. The sooner he offloaded the house, the better. Only bad and bitter memories remained here.

'Please,' Peter said and Hank nodded his agreement.

Roy booked three taxis and then turned to Peter: 'Erm, about Livvy's ashes – when we get them, Hank would like to take half to LA for a memorial service and internment. She was very much loved on the US country music scene and it's only fitting there should be some sort of tribute so her fans can pay their last respects. Is that okay with you?' He'd managed to keep the details of the close family funeral quiet today, for the sake of Harley and Courtney, although the press had somehow got wind and no doubt it would be on every TV news channel that night. They'd have to organise a fans' memorial service at a later date in the UK too.

Peter nodded. 'We'll have a family service for our side back at home and scatter the rest of her ashes in the Garden of Remembrance at our local church.' He looked at Harley and Courtney: 'You girls are more than welcome to visit us any time, you know.'

Courtney smiled wearily. 'And we will do, Grandpa. Jamie and I plan to "do" Scotland sometime soon.'

'When Harley's feeling up to it, we'll bring the babies for a visit,' Jack said.

Roy was worried about Harley. She'd hardly spoken a word since the accident and that bothered him. She'd been making such good progress too. He went into the kitchen and stood by the French window, remembering the first time he'd looked across the gardens with Livvy when they first viewed Ashlea Grange. Danny had been a new baby and the girls in their mid-teens. Livvy had loved the house from the start and he recalled how happy she'd been at that time. He'd tried, he'd really tried, to be everything she wanted him to be, but his heart was never truly in it; Sammy had been the one to hold his heart and his soul and always would be. He was sorry it had all come to this.

He wondered what had made Livvy lose her mind towards the end. She had everything going for her – her new husband, who clearly adored her, even though she couldn't seem to see it, or refused to see it more like, an upturn in her own and Juice's popularity, and her kids. But she'd started drinking a couple of years ago and that hadn't helped. Peter had taken him to one side the previous night, when Sammy had cooked a meal for everyone at Jasmine House, and told him in confidence that Gina suffered from depression and that she'd spent some time in a mental institution following the birth of Livvy. He hinted that maybe Livvy's mood swings might be something to do with RJ's birth. It was his opinion that she'd not been quite right since then and had found RJ hard to cope with.

Roy had agreed. He told Peter he'd had concerns over Livvy's impatient attitude with RJ.

'Ah well,' Peter had finished, patting him on the shoulder, 'at least those wee laddies will have all the stability in the world with you and your wife – she's very good with them.'

Roy agreed. 'She adores them. You and Gina will always be welcome at Jasmine House. You're the only grandparents my kids have got. Please don't be strangers.'

Peter's eyes had filled. 'That'll make Gina very happy. She's worried to death about losing contact with them.'

Roy lit a cigarette and opened the French door. No matter what reasons they all gave for Livvy's behaviour, it didn't excuse what she'd done to Jon and Jess. Jon was currently staying at

Sean and Tina's place. He'd been over to Jasmine House a few times to ask advice on how to make things right. Jane and Eddie had talked to both Jess and Jon and now at least the pair were speaking and Jon was still taking his turn at helping with the babies. Roy was certain Jess would allow him home in time. The pair still loved one another very much and at least she knew now that Livvy had been lying about her and Jon screwing around. She was still finding it hard to come to terms with his one-night stand with Sheena but time was a good healer and the pair had a lot going for them. They'd work it through eventually. A lot of lessons had been learnt in the last few years. Older and wiser, that was a good saying, and so true. A loud tooting of car horns broke his daydreams and Roy threw the butt of his cigarette onto the patio and locked the French doors.

He saw everyone out to the taxis and promised to be in touch. 'Tell your mum I'll be about half an hour,' he said to Harley.

Back indoors, he poured another drink and sat on the sofa. He could feel his eyes filling. It had been an emotional day, an emotional last three weeks. Whatever she'd become, Livvy had given him beautiful kids and his life was a lot richer for them. He hoped she was finally at peace now.

* * *

Sammy settled Harley and the others in the lounge and brought in a tray of sandwiches and drinks. 'The boys are in bed early,' she said. 'I thought you might like a little peaceful time to yourselves.'

'Thank you, Sammy,' Courtney said. 'We appreciate it.'

Sammy left them to it and went to sit in the kitchen to wait for Roy. When he came in, she put her arms around him. He looked drained. She sat him down and pushed a mug of coffee towards him.

'Thanks, Sam. I'm glad to get out of that place. It felt so weird. I don't ever want to go back there – the estate agent and solicitor can deal with things from now on.'

'You just have to look to the future,' Sammy said. 'We've got a lovely family, great and supportive friends and everything to look forward to. I think we've acquired another daughter too. Courtney's rootless, poor girl. Her sister and brothers are here. I guess we should tell her she can make this place her base for when she's not travelling.'

'Aw, Sam, I was going to suggest that to you. Thanks, darling. She's called me Dad a few times in the past.'

Sammy smiled. 'End of one era and the start of another. RJ called me Mummy tonight and Danny copied him. They were all giggly about it.'

'And do you mind being called Mummy?'

'Not at all – I love it, I feel quite honoured.'

'That nice peaceful retirement we were looking forward to seems further away than ever,' Roy said with a sigh.

'We can't retire. Who wants to anyway? We'd be bored stiff. We're not quite old codgers yet. You're taking The Raiders out on the road again soon and unleashing Nathan onto your unsuspecting fans. That should be fun for you. And I'm going to enjoy our grandchildren, look after our little boys and take care of Harley. Just like old times.'

'I'll drink to old times.' Roy clinked his coffee mug with hers and smiled. 'Just wish we were forty years younger!'

A LETTER FROM PAM

Dear reader,

I want to say a huge thank you for choosing to read *Dreams on Mersey Square*. If you did enjoy it, and want to keep up to date with all my latest releases, just sign up at the following link. Your email address will never be shared and you can unsubscribe at any time.

www.bookouture.com/pam-howes

To my loyal band of regular readers who bought and reviewed all my previous stories, thank you for waiting patiently for another book. Your support is most welcome and very much appreciated.

As always, a big thank you to Beverley Ann Hopper and Sandra Blower and the members of their Facebook group, Book Lovers. Thanks for all the support you show me. Also, thank you to Deryl Easton and the supportive members of her Facebook group, Gangland Governors/NotRights.

A huge thank you to team Bookouture, especially my lovely editor Maisie Lawrence. As always, it's been such a pleasure to work with you again, and thanks also to copyeditor/line editor Jane Eastgate and proofreader Jane Donovan for the copy edits and proofreading side of life.

And last, but definitely not least, thank you to our amazing media team, Kim Nash, Sarah Hardy, Jess Readett and Noelle

Holton for everything you do for us. You're 'Simply the Best' as Tina would say! And thanks also to the gang in the Bookouture Authors' Lounge for always being there. As always, I'm so proud to be one of you.

I hope you loved *Dreams on Mersey Square* and if you did, I would be very grateful if you could write a review. I'd love to hear what you think and it makes such a difference helping new readers to discover one of my books for the first time.

I love hearing from my readers – you can get in touch on my Facebook page or through Twitter.

Thanks,

Pam Howes

facebook.com/Pam-Howes-Books-260328010709267

x.com/PamHowes1

ACKNOWLEDGEMENTS

As always, for my partner, my daughters, grandchildren, great-granddaughters and all their partners/spouses. Thanks for being a supportive and lovely family.